Once
Upon a
Woman

EMMA NWANERI

authorHOUSE®

AuthorHouse™
1663 Liberty Drive
Bloomington, IN 47403
www.authorhouse.com
Phone: 1 (800) 839-8640

Published by AuthorHouse 11/10/2015

ISBN: 978-1-5049-6173-8 (sc)
ISBN: 978-1-5049-6172-1 (e)

Print information available on the last page.

*Any people depicted in stock imagery provided by Thinkstock are models,
and such images are being used for illustrative purposes only.
Certain stock imagery © Thinkstock.*

This book is printed on acid-free paper.

*Scripture quotations marked KJV are from the Holy Bible, King James
Version (Authorized Version). First published in 1611. Quoted from the KJV
Classic Reference Bible, Copyright © 1983 by The Zondervan Corporation.*

CONTENTS

PROLOGUE

OROGWE, EASTERN NIGERIA, 1968

"A voice was heard in Ramah, lamentation and bitter weeping; Rachel weeping for her children, refused to be comforted for her children, because they were not"
- Jeremiah 31:15

The congregation spilled out reluctantly into the pouring rain, all of them trailing behind the singing choristers; they also following the lone, white-clad figure of the presiding minister. It was a rain-drenched Indian file of grief.

Dressed from head to toe in matching black clothes, Chinedum Okoroafor walked as if in a trance. He refused to look up as the congregation weaved its way out of the small, cold church building into the colder, wet courtyard that served as both a car park and a cemetery. It was the cemetery that the group of mourners, friends, family and clergy were all headed to as the heavens released a constant stream of light but persistent rain.

All around him, people were shuffling impatiently and irritably; mumbling and singing along with the choir the dirge chosen for the occasion.

Chinedum moved on mechanically, chewing on his lips.

Ahead of the minister, the pall-bearers had by now arrived at the freshly-dug grave. Covered in brown mackintosh raincoats, they were stationed, all six of them around the gaping hole that was soon to swallow the mahogany coffin they had just carried out of the church several minutes back.

Sadness accompanied the ceaseless rain in generous quantity and spread amongst the soaked group slowly approaching the grave. The singing apart, no one said a word. No one could. The funeral they were all witnesses to was as painful and heartbreaking as any in living memory. This funeral especially was an exercise in misery.

Who could believe that such a sad event could be taking place?

None, among all those gathered could understand how fate could have played such a mindless trick in so cruel a manner as to turn an extravagantly-planned wedding into a grief-stricken funeral? How? How on earth could this be happening when just a few days ago, everyone was involved in the arrangements for a grand wedding?

Chinedum saw nothing and heard nothing happening around him. All he saw was wet, brown mud crunched under the sole of his shoes. His mind was too numbed to take notice of anything else. Surely it wasn't him here. No way could it be him. Yes, the person clothed in the dark shirt, tucked into black matching pants looked like him, but his frozen mind refused to accept that it was him standing here in the rain burying his beloved. Burying Anjola.

Someone nudged him in the small of his back.

He didn't react; still pretending it wasn't him there. Possibly, just by some small chance if he stood still enough and ignored everything around him, he could wake up from this nightmare and be free at last. Be free to be with his beautiful, childlike Anjola.

The small jolt came again. This time, stronger than the first.

"Don't just stand there looking gormless, we are all waiting for you", a voice whispered in Igbo.

The middle-aged minister it was who had been nudging him. Chinedum had known him since he was a seven year-old, being dragged to church by his mother. Then, he was a young, handsome man just out of the seminary. Glancing at him now in the deluge, he hardly recognized him anymore as the same catechist who rained down prophecies of fire and brimstone to all sinners, from his enormous altar.

Betraying his growing exasperation, he grabbed Chinedum by the arm; dragging him forward and shoving the wet handle of a shovel into his hands.

So it was true. It wasn't a dream at all. It was reality. Anjola was gone.

What was that verse in the Holy Book about Rachel crying for her lost children? Rachel who could not be comforted? Chinedum felt very much like Rachel at this moment. Depression weighed heavily like a millstone all around him.

He wanted to join his beloved inside the mahogany coffin. Surely there would be space for two in the casket. Inside there, lying beside his sweet, angelic Anjola, he knew he would be happier. He knew he would find joy beside her slender, saintly body. The body he had held so severally, so delicately, so lovingly, so many nights.

The pitty-patter of the rain, now drumming on the surface of the casket was melancholic music to his ears. Music inviting him to move closer and yank open the heavy lid and squeeze himself inside; beside his beloved.

"Nedum", the gruff, well-nourished voice of the minister intruded into his thoughts again.

"Nedum", he whispered conspiratorially, "we are all freezing out here. Please commence the rites so we bury her in peace and leave".

The rites, as is common in that part of Eastern Nigeria, was that the chief mourner in a funeral was expected to throw the first lump of earth on the coffin of the deceased.

Him to throw dirt on Anjola? Him? Anjola? How could he?

He would rather....out of the corner of his eyes, he glimpsed a couple of the pallbearers staring at him, looking slightly angry. He couldn't blame them. Surely, the poor bastards must be freezing to death.

Someone clasped another wet, stronger hand over his, making it a double grip on the now-slippery handle of the shovel. It was one of the pallbearers obviously trying to urge him to pick up soil from the edge of the grave and dump it on the coffin. He wriggled free from the man's nicotine-stained fingers and moved trance-like towards the grave. Towards Anjola. All the time, he kept on chewing his tortured lips.

Around him, the singing had stopped. Soaked to the skin, all eyes were now trained on him. Waiting for him to make a move. To set the ball rolling. To bring this sad sequence of events to a speedy end.

He took another step forward. Towards the grave. Towards Anjola. Everyone watched him like a hawk watches a prey. Willing him forward in their minds. He knew they all couldn't wait to see the dead buried and they return to the warmth of their various homes. To see Anjola submerged and covered up in this watery grave, while they all recoiled back into their cosy homes. Back to their comfortable lives and carry on as if all was normal again. Poor, innocent Anjola. About to be left alone in this sepulcher of darkness. Alone in a chamber six feet under the earth with no company. No *warmth. Not even her favourite hot chocolate to keep away the chill. Nothing. Just by herself. Surrounded by silence, darkness and walls of peeling soil.*

No, he couldn't do this to her. His precious Anjola. No he couldn't.

He took another step. This time, more resolute. Then another step.

The rain fell relentlessly. As if trying to tell him something. As if saying that it wouldn't stop falling until Anjola either rose up and walked out of that damn wooden box; or he joined her in it.

He took two steps now. Firmer, stiffer, with renewed purpose. Heads raised all around him with relief. Soon, they sensed, this would be over and they could all retreat inside – out of this bone-chilling rain.

The minister followed closely behind, watching Chinedum as he moved closer to the huge, gaping hole that would serve as Anjola's last, resting place. He reached the periphery of the grave. He could see over the edge now. It wasn't as deep as he thought it would be. Inside, resting on concrete tripods was the casket. Already a small pool of water could be seen beneath it. The ceaseless rain had formed a bed of water and if he didn't hurry up, the coffin could soon be floating. Just like Noah's ark. Except that this ark contained no living things.

He halted by the grave. From when the minister had first nudged him till now, he had taken only seven steps to get to the edge of the grave. It felt like a great trek. Weary in mind and even more-fatigued physically, Chinedum told himself he had to summon all the reserves of his strength to do this final deed.

He stooped forward, picked up a clump of wet soil with the shovel and heaved it onto the top of the coffin. A muted murmur went through the gathered audience behind him. He thought he heard someone say Amen.

He bent forward again as if to scoop up another load of soil.

Instead, he pitched headlong into grave, landing on top of the casket in a heap.

Shouts rang from above him. He could hear all manner of noises and screams. Raised voices yelled at him. At other people. At themselves.

Some called out his name. Asking him what on earth he thought he was doing. Someone threw a rope at him, urging him to grab it and hoist himself out of the grave. All around and above him, pandemonium broke out.

The solemn congregation that had been huddling silently around the grave suddenly transformed into a helter-skelter rabble. People running in all directions. People spreading around the entire perimeter of the grave, peering inside to behold this most-unbelievable of sights. Mayhem, bedlam reigned.

Everyone was caught totally unaware by the sudden turn of events. Everyone, except of course the youngman now lying breathlessly, spread-eagled across the coffin, frantically attempting to prise it open by the thick edges.

Realising that the lid of the coffin would not budge, Chinedum fiercely looked around him in the grave for something, anything to help him in his angry task. He could only find the edge of the thick rope thrown at him moments earlier. Frustrated, he used his bare fingers to pry loose rocks and stones from the side of the grave, hoping one of them would be big enough to aid him.

Meanwhile, shouting and cursing alike continued above him. A couple of the pallbearers were readying themselves to jump in and drag him out of the grave. He sensed what was coming next and braced himself.

"No, No!", he yelled, looking up at the stunned hitherto-mourners. "Leave me alone let me die with my wife!".

"I'm not leaving this grave. I'm not. Nobody must come inside here...bury me with her. Oh, bury me with her! Can't you all hear me? I said bury me. Let them cover me also with the soil! It is ok! It is my wish! I'm not leaving here, never!!"

Before anyone else could react, two of the pallbearers jumped in and seized Chinedum by the hands. Initially they planned on calming him down and try to persuade him to give up this manic, suicide attempt. But soon as they joined him in the now-mushy grave, he attacked them.

They were both sturdy men used to rough work but Chinedum's animal strength surprised them. He punched one of them squarely in the stomach and clobbered the other in the face with his other arm. The first man staggered around drunkily for a second, while the other evaded Chinedum's wild blows.

Above them, people screamed their encouragement, urging the men to grab Chinedum. It was a sight beyond anyone's wildest thinking.

One of the men finally remembered the swinging rope thrown at Chinedum moments earlier. He sneaked onto it and while his partner distracted Chinedum, he stole behind him and lassoed him from behind. The second man, facing Chinedum moved in fast and they wrapped thick arms round him, amidst an almighty struggle with the rope, circling it round and round his twisting body.

"Let me go! Let me go! Leave me to die here! I want to die here!", he repeated breathlessly to no avail. The combined strength of both men proved too much for him to overcome. More men jumped into the ruined grave to offer helping *hands and in the midst of all the commotion and scuffle, one of them mistakenly hit their prey on the head.*

Chinedum, grappling feebly at empty air, collapsed into the men's arms as they lifted his supine body up into more waiting arms stretched out along the grave.

Soon as they brought him out of the grave, the anguished catechist said his final prayers for the soul of the departed and the coffin was promptly submerged under a barrage of black clay.

Everyone departed hurriedly from the graveside. As if something sinister would happen again to further drag this ill-fated funeral on. One of the mourners' vehicles was quickly commandeered to convey Chinedum's still-unconscious figure to his mother's home which was on the other side of the village.

Almost two hours later, when he emerged from coma, he was to realise much to his distress, that he was still very much alive – separated forever from the woman he had loved like his own skin.

Beautiful Anjola Badmus.

JOHANNESBURG, SOUTH AFRICA, 1999

CHAPTER ONE

In the land of blind men, the one-eyed man is king

"Do you know what his name is?", she asked the class.

No one responded.

"I mean can anyone tell me the name of the English writer known for the use of tautology in his writings?"

Still no response from the class of about 35 students.

Slightly embarrassed, Ms Angelou now considered calling out names. She hated doing this because now if she asked any particular student to give an answer, and they failed to do so, it would mean she had to keep calling out more names until someone got it right. The students didn't like it either.

It was a lunchtime class in Contemporary African Literature and they were treating one of Athol Fugard's plays, *Master Harold and the Boys*, when someone noted that Fugard's plot sometimes had similarities with English playwrights.

Could it mean no one of all the 35-odd numbskulls sitting facing her, were paying attention to her since the start of the class half an hour ago?

"Ok, Ms....", a half-confident voice rang out. She snapped to attention, seeking out the voice like a stowaway reaching for a rescuer.

"Yes? Who..?", the question died on her lips as Angelou searched out the owner of the voice.

"Ms Angelou", the voice repeated again, this time more audibly.

It was coming from the direction of the door, which led into the classroom and it belonged to Rupert, who often always came late because he claimed, he had to take four buses before getting to the campus everyday.

Angelou turned in his direction with relief that someone at last would bail her out of her predicament before thirty-five, searching pairs of eyes.

"Ok Rupert, you know my rules concerning late coming to my classes, but we'll deal with that later, what.....do you have an answer for us?"

"Yes, Ms Angelou, I think it is Samuel Johnson"

Angelou sighed a huge sigh of relief. In all her fifteen-and-half years of teaching European Literature and Classical Poetry, she thought she had seen all kinds of students in the hallways and lecture rooms of the two universities she had taught in. Until this gangling, care-free man of about two dozen years-old enrolled in the department about three years back.

"So can you please give us any examples of his use of tautology?", she pondered at him.

"Ok, yes he was the one who re-phrased the saying, birds of the same feather flock together", Rupert responded.

"Into what?", she asked for the benefit of the rest of them

"He changed it to, natural aeroplanes of identical plumage congregate in the nearest proximity", he declared smoothly.

"That is so clever of you", she announced as a round of impressive clapping broke out.

Rupert Mabizela was what you could call an anti-student. That was because he appeared like everything a student ought not to be. A serious student that is. He of course always arrived late from home. No one ever saw him around the campus, or in the various places and rendezvous where students loved to hang out and while away the time. He arrived late and vanished to wherever he emerges from as soon as his mission for the day was accomplished. He truly justified the phrase that appearances could be deceptive.

Often casually-dressed in rolled-up long sleeved shirts; tail shirt flapping behind fading Levis, he looked very much the way he was attired. Casual to a fault and everlastingly carefree. He had a few friends among the young men in his department, but all of them would tell you they knew as much about him as a magpie knew about the submarine lifestyle of a mackerel. It was like being friends with the wind. Can't see enough of it to grab hold of, least of all strike up an acquaintance.

Rupert was almost always in a hurry. Never one to stand still for too long, he was forever on the move. When not breezing in and out of lectures, he was scribbling on his folded Higher Education notebook; darting in and out of offices, or in search of someone or something. If you've ever heard the expression 'an orang-outang on anti-depressants', it's Rupert. Hyperactive. Restless. All-action.

If such a reputation bothered him, he never showed it. Actually, he didn't care. He just went about his business and turned his nose up at the rest of the world.

His attitude nonetheless had very little effect on his studies. If any at all. He was simply put, a top scholar. Brilliant seemed an inadequate word to describe him. He was an outstanding genius. Not only was he the best student in the entire 300Level of the Dramatic Arts department, he even helped out several of his seniors in their final year assignments and projects. A voracious reader, he could recite most poems from memory.

John Milton's famous *Paradise Lost* was a bible of sorts for most literature majors in the department and everyone dreaded it. Everyone that is, except Mr Mabizela. He not only freely read out the lengthy, complex poem line by line, he had equally mastered the lines of its sequel, *Paradise Regained.* It was an unwritten rule that you could not hope to graduate with good grades without committing some part of Milton 's epic to memory. Rupert did more than that. Since dissecting both works of Milton, he had taken on Chaucer's *Canterbury Tales*, which was a no-go area for his mates.

To everyone's utter amazement, Rupert could also easily work out mathematical problems mentally, in the time it took most students to grab a seat and open their books. Many wondered why he was 'wasting' his talents in studying Drama and Literature. A broad consensus among his peers was that he wouldn't have been out of place majoring in Medicine. Or Aeronautic Engineering. Or even Kinetics. Such was the awe in which they held him. In their admiring eyes, he was like a king.

But Miss Angelou was grateful to tutor such a brilliant student. As one of the more-experienced lecturers in the department, she recognized the shining light someone like Rupert represented and understood quite early that he was a special student. She had taught him and his mates in six different courses since their Year one and looked forward to supervising Rupert's final year project in the next session.

Though she wished he could tidy up his appearance a bit more, she still accepted that so often every genius came along with a flaw. So a dress code – or lack of it - might just be his only undoing. Just as she always taught her students, every hero needed a villain to draw attention to himself.

Well, you couldn't tell young people of today what to, and what not to do. Not even if they were students in your class. The world now was a much more different place than she knew it when she was their age almost two decades back.

They all accorded her great respect and held her in high regard. Not just students alone but her colleague-lecturers. Despite her status as a single, middle-aged woman who never married and never had children of her own, everyone around treated her with deference. They all admired her calm, motherly mien and took her words with grave seriousness. Very few, if any knew about her private life. She guarded that jealously and it had worked to create a halo around her over the years she had been in the university.

Students and fellow-teachers alike saw her as some kind of Mother Theresa who spread good cheer, tender loving care, warmth and wisdom everywhere she went. Her profile was so high even among her colleagues that rumour had been making the rounds for sometime that she was being considered to replace the aging Professor Benson Nomvete, head of the department who was retiring at the end of the academic session.

If she had heard the rumours, Angelou never betrayed any emotion. As always she took everything in her stride and rolled along with the days and months.

All these of course did not give her the right to correct any student's dress style. In the *laissez-faire* world of tertiary education, boundaries of personal freedom were invisible but strictly maintained.

Still, Angelou could never get over the feeling that the whipper-snapper genius embodied inside Rupert 'needed'

5

her careful attention to nurture. The more she had seen him over the past three years, the more she was drawn to him. He looked sometimes to her, like a lost soul. A lone petrel searching for something even he himself did not know. Like some missing link in huge, mammoth puzzle. Though she always felt ashamed to admit it, even to herself, she longed to be the verger to his whimsical passions.

Over time, she had come to the realization that she wanted to watch over him.

Oh stop it, she often told herself. I'm sure he has a good mother whom he goes home to everyday from school and she definitely fawns over him. She often found herself wondering about his background. He looked like someone from good stock. His polite and deliberate manners suggested that. Unlike most of his mates, she had never seen a cigarette dangling from his fingers or a bottle hidden in a paper bag. More interestingly to her, he never seemed to be found in female company. She had carefully noticed over the years, that he was one of the last to arrive for lectures and almost the first to leave the class. He seemed not to be interested in the many girls who yearned for his attention and wanted to be seen with him. To her surprise relief, apart from some polite small talk and explanations of school work, he always found an excuse not to be with girls.

Or, could he be gay? She had thought of it but after another period of close observation, she had dismissed that possibility. All the subtle signs were absent. Not for him tight, skinny pants. Or elaborate hand motions when talking. Or a fake accent. Or feminine eye movements. He looked every bit a full-blooded man.

For the past twenty-six years, 45year-old Angelou had lived a life of deliberate denial. Suppressing her personal grief and desires to pour herself into her work and become the icon she now was in the university world and among South Africa 's learned circles. It had been a long, lonely road of rejection. A road she had chosen to travel alone. A road she believed she would remain on till her last breath. A soulless journey of constant pain; pain again and again. A life she had allowed no one to have a look-in. Not even Maria. Not anyone. Faithful Maria knew only half of her story.

It was a cross she had resigned herself to carrying on her own.

All these sufficed until three years ago when Rupert Mabizela enrolled in her department and since that late spring morning, a strange restlessness had overcome her.

Something about him reminded her of her lost life. Something about this languid yokelling stirred up her hidden past. She sensed deeply and disturbingly that the calm, orderly waters of her life were about to be disturbed.

CHAPTER TWO

My humanity is bound up in yours – Archbishop Desmond Tutu.

It was just past noon but Angelou knew she wasn't going to make it through the rest of the day.

Although she had a crucial meeting with a couple of graduating students who wanted to discuss final details of their project work, she just couldn't wait for all that anymore.

Already she could sense the beginnings of a splitting headache.

"Hey, Angel why don't you come with me to the blue room?", a blonde head appeared at the door of her office.

"No ways Maria. Not sure I can make it through the day. My head is splitting in two".

"Come on you old girl', Maria teased her. "You need to get out more and stop locking yourself indoors"

"Hey, I just finished three hours with those second year kids. I sure need some break"

"You'll get the break in the blue room. Come on, let's go", Maria persisted.

Angelou knew she wouldn't take No for answer.

She was always like that. Maria Van Dyke. Her best friend. Confidant. Agony-aunt. Co-lecturer. All rolled into one. At 53, she was like an older sister to Angelou and reminded her a lot of her aunt whom she hadn't seen in twenty-nine years.

The eight, odd years difference between them was often blurred as Angelou accepted the older woman's friendship and company with trust and complete dependence. There was hardly anything about herself she didn't share with Maria. Herself a divorcee, she had coveted and cherished Angelou's company and presence in her life since their paths crossed almost eight years ago. As lecturers in the Dramatic Arts Department of University of Johannesburg, their work drew them naturally together.

Maria was just coming out of an unpleasant, sour divorce with her husband of nine years when they met in the winter of 1994. Maria, then a research fellow at the highly-rated University of Stellenbosch was using facilities at the Johannesburg University for some of her work and therefore spent a lot of time in the city. Her prolonged absence from home in Stellenbosch, on the other side of the country in the Western Cape, afforded her husband time to strike up and nurture an illicit relationship.

Maria was at the tail end of her one-year research work, when she discovered his unfaithfulness. They fought bitterly over it and though he admitted his guilt and pleaded with her for forgiveness, it was too late to save the marriage. The other woman was already six months heavy with child for Maria's husband and childless Maria found herself losing out.

Heartbroken and confused, she returned to Johannesburg to round up her research preparatory to filing for divorce. Completing her work of referencing which was the final part of the project proved even too much. Every where she looked, the young face of her rival with her protruding stomach, carrying Gary's unborn child confronted her. She wept bucket loads and slipped daily into a cesspit of depression.

It was in such a position – head bowed on a reading table inside the confines of the Gertrude Posel art gallery at the nearby Witswatersrand University, with tears flowing freely – that Angelou found her one cold night in August, 1994.

The year itself was a watershed in South Africa's history.

The troubled nation had just emerged from almost 100years of hateful segregration along racial lines. 'Madiba' Nelson Mandela had negotiated a peaceful end to apartheid and though there was euphoria across the nation, only the newly-free black people truly felt the excitement. All over the huge country, *"Amandla"* was the word. People saw 1994 as the dawn of a brand new era. The beginning of a real life. The start of a new, promising chapter in their harrowing history. The birth of a nation of hope. For the black people – oppressed and marginalized for a century – 1994 was the realization of the dream of a lifetime of struggle.

For most of the white people however, the opposite was the case. Their forefathers had seized the land from its original black owners and exploited both its resources and people for their personal gain. They had done this through force, intimidation and blood-letting. Undiluted hatred was the only phrase to describe the relationship that therefore existed between blacks and white for over a century.

In 1994 however, the tables turned with the end of apartheid. An election held over three days in April marked the birth of a new land. A new country which Archbishop Desmond Tutu famously coined as the 'Rainbow Nation'.

For most white South Africans however, 1994 wasn't the dawn of anything new. It was for them, the beginning of the end. Or so they thought. Despite the best efforts of Mandela and his fellow freedom fighters, they feared a bitter, hate-filled backlash from the majority, angry black people.

It was however not to be. Commonsense prevailed and Mandela, himself a major victim of aggravated injustice and denial, prevailed upon his fellow-blacks not to seek vengeance. In what proved to be a monumental example to the rest of the world, they heeded his advice and embraced their erstwhile oppressors.

The whole world watched in amazement – and admiration.

Tutu again captured the moment best with his famous statement that, "My humanity is bound up in yours. For we can only be human together".

Naturally however, suspicion still reigned between the different races. Nearly 100 years of master-servant relationship couldn't be wished away by Mandela's oratorical skills.

It was this situation that prevailed everywhere in the new, rainbow nation when black Angelou encountered white Maria that fateful evening in a gallery hallway of the Wits University. Clearly, it was an awkward scene.

The sight of a distressed white woman looking up to a very composed, black companion for comfort. In South Africa, white people were not known or seen to be in anguish. They were rather known and seen to have it all. Wealth, good jobs, education, nice homes, comfort, everything. They were the epitome of contentment and happiness.

Even if for any reason they found themselves in need, it wasn't the place of their poor, black 'subjects' to provide them succour. It just didn't happen in fragmented South Africa.

But it did happen that night.

From complete strangers, Angelou and Maria broke down the walls of suspicion and mistrust to bond excellently and sow the seeds of a deep, symbiotic acquaintance. The younger black woman had walked into the life of the older, white woman at a time the latter most-needed the support and ears of someone. Just anybody.

All that happened five years ago, but it remained as poignant and powerful in both their minds. Especially Maria's.

They finally got to the Blue Room; so-called because its four walls and 250 leather seats were all covered in blue. In truth, it was an amphitheatre which the staff and students of the Arts faculties used for staging plays, recitals, rehearsals and all manner of entertainment that happened to form part of their work.

Today, stand-up comedy was the sole item on the menu.

CHAPTER THREE

A good sense of humour is the pole that adds balance to the tightrope of life.

"Can anyone tell me the name of the only animal which can read a book?", Napoleon asked the audience.

Silence greeted him.

"Anyone? Anybody?"

No one was sure if Napoleon was his real name or not, but everyone called him that around the campus. He was billed as tonight's main attraction and by the time Angelou with Maria walked into the blue room, he was already warming up the crowd.

"Yes? Anybody with the answer? Hey com'on everyone, this is a uni-ver-sity with the best brains in the country. Don't let yourselves down", he proclaimed with a cheeky smile.

A murmur spread through the crowd. No one had a clue what the answer could be.

"Ok, let me encourage you all. If anyone gives me the answer, I will buy them lunch tomorrow at Campos Square. If I give the answer, everyone here buys me lunch for the next one month. Agreed?"

Yet another murmur. Some voices rose up from the back yelling their agreement to the lopsided deal. No one knew the answer anyway so Napoleon could as well have his way.

"Ok, if you all agree with me, can I then pass a paper around for everyone to put down their names so I know who's buying me lunch and what day?".

True to his words, he produced a sheet of paper from his jacket and gave it to someone in the front row to pass it on.

"Now that's cool. Ok, when the list comes back to me, I'll give you the answer", he announced triumphantly, rubbing his hands together in mock glee.

"Now, let's start with a short story", he feigned seriousness, prancing around the stage.

"While waiting for a flight at an airport terminal", he began, "former US President George Bush saw an old man with a long white beard, holding a long staff. Approaching him, George Bush asked, 'Are you not Moses who parted the Red Sea and led the Israelites from Egypt?' The old man ignored him. George Bush asked him the second time, but the man still remained silent. Determined, President Bush asked for the third time and at last, the old man responded. "I'll rather not answer, because the last time I spoke to a bush, I spent the next 40years in the wilderness!"

The entire hall burst into raucous laughter. Angelou joined in the amusement. Sitting to her right in the dimly-lit room, Maria was straining at her sides with a suppressed laugh threatening to break out from her lips.

Napoleon had that effect on everyone. He was as famous as his jokes and today was no exception. A master of the art of stand-up humour, he was in his elements tonight.

"Ok, everybody, calm down, calm down", he resumed, raising his voice above the general din.

"Let's go again. A dairy farmer went into an electrical store to buy a CCTV system for monitoring his cows. Thinking of making a fast deal, the store attendant tried talking him into purchasing a state-of-the-art, coloured system, if he could add a few extra cash. After listening patiently to the attendant, the farmer responded. "I won't be needing that, because I've only got black and white cows!"

Once again there was uproar. General laughter coupled with raised voices exploded through the hall. Napoleon paced around the stage as if oblivious to what was going on below him.

He merely grinned, hands folded behind his back and nodded his head continuously like a redneck lizard.

"Don't forget to pass the list around, please", he reminded the audience with a wide smile. After those two jokes, he sure merited breakfast, lunch and dinner from everyone in the room.

When the uproar subsided, Napoleon again went on the offensive.

"A woman and her five year-old daughter went to the cemetery to lay flowers on the grave of their late granny. As they were leaving the cemetery, they passed another grave on which was written the words. 'Here Lies a Lawyer and a Good Man'. Obviously confused, the little girl looked up and asked her mother, 'Mum, do they now bury two people in one grave?!'

The hall erupted again. Scores of people rose from their seats, clapping, cheering and applauding all at the same time.

The man at the centre of it all, Napoleon, seemed oblivious to all the excitement below him as he strolled leisurely across the stage, with a wicked smile on his funny face.

Maria and Angelou were in fits as well as most of the other people in the audience.

"Ok, ok everybody", Napoleon sang out. "I hope my list is completed. It should be coming back to me now", he added, smiling through it all.

Fully revved-up now, he unleashed more and more jokes on the audience.

There was the one about a man who swallowed 120 coins over a bet and got admitted to the hospital. Doctors monitoring his situation said so far, 'no change'.

There was another one about a snake who wrote a love letter to its girlfriend and signed it off at the end: 'With Love and Hisses!'

His jokes were punctuated with witty one-liners such as: 'The problem isn't that there are problems in life. The problem is expecting no problem and thinking that having problems is a problem'.

His repertoire was inexhaustible and kept his audience baying for more.

The wisecracks kept rolling off his lips, sending the crowd into fits of laughter and making them yell for more. No one in the room wanted him to stop. He sensed their mood and after lifting them all up to a frenzied climax, he announced that he would be calling it a day but not before getting his list back, after which he would give them the answer to the riddle.

After a slight delay of some few minutes, the list was returned to him onstage and pretending to scrutinize it first, he pocketed it with a satisfied smile and then cunnily asked his audience again.

"Can anyone remind me the riddle again?"

Several voices yelled back the question to him.

"Oh, ok I remember now. Yes, it's about which animal can read, right?"

"Oh it is quite simple", he teased them. "I'm surprised no one in this citadel of knowledge could tell me. Anyway, the answer isssss............"

".....a bookworm!"

Gasps of disbelief went round, eventually erupting into another round of laughter, clapping and cheering during which Napoleon executed an elaborate bow to the commotion below before making his exit.

As the excited crowd trooped out of the blue room amidst a noisy chatter, Angelou, still clutching Maria's arm realized to her relief that her looming headache had disappeared.

CHAPTER FOUR

Little drops of water make the ocean mighty

There was a knock on her office door.

She didn't hear it the first time as she shuffled files and papers into her hold-all, preparatory to calling it a day. It had been a long day. Longer than usual because the lecturers had all been closeted in the Head of Department's office in a marathon meeting. The department was planning for its annual week, during which several activities had been lined-up. Many of those activities involved lectures, a seminar, drama presentations, film shows, group photos with several invited personalities and a dinner at the Great Hall to round up the week.

Angelou, as co-chairman of the week's planning committee, was heavily involved in all the arrangements. She had sat through two other meetings after the one with the HOD, which was why her day had extended so late.

Looking forward to the drive home and a warm bath, she couldn't wait to leave the office and call it a day.

The knock came again. This time it startled her.

"Yes, who's there?"

"Oh it's me Maam". It was the HOD's female secretary. "I finally found the phone numbers you requested and made them up into a list for you. Here..."

She had asked the young lady to find the phone numbers of some of the people they were inviting for the activities of the week. She had actually forgotten all about it amidst all the avalanche of work she had to deal with.

"Oh thank you very much my dear. That was thoughtful of you".

She quickly scanned the list and to her amazement found that there were over thirty numbers there. How on earth would she ever get around to making thirty phonecalls along with the mountain of other work she had to do as well?

Then an idea struck her.

"My dear", she addressed the lady who was about leaving, "do you think you can help me call those numbers and tell them the dates of our programmes and secure their invitations? I'm so tied up with lots of work and I need someone to help".

"Ok Maam, I can do that for you, but some of them are really important people and they may prefer to talk to you..."

'That is ok, if they need me, just transfer the calls to my office and I'll talk to them directly".

The secretary was right.

Some on the list were quite important people in commerce, cultural circles, academia and even in government. There were company CEOs, playwrights, high-ups in government on the list but most of them were on first name basis with her and she had no doubt they would honour her with their presence.

Legends like John Kani; television executives like Kethiwe Ndugane; corporate barons and many other names too numerous to single out.

They all knew her and she had cordial relationships with them dating over ten years.

The annual week was just three weeks away and there was still so much to do. Venues to be booked; participants, speakers to be officially informed; invitations to be sent out; students of the department to be mobilized. This wasn't the first time she had been involved with the planning of such event, but it was the first time she was being put directly in-charge.

With the help of Maria and several other lecturers however things moved at a good pace.

"You know what Angel, the HOD gave me some names of people he invited for the programme", Maria disclosed later that evening as she sat across from Angelou in the latter's loungeroom. "Most of them are from overseas... y'know from places like Botswana, Namibia and Nigeria. Here, I think I've got it in my bag".

While rummaging through her brown Yves St Laurent bag, Maria didn't notice the frozen look on her friend's face. The mention of Nigeria had hit her below the belt. Though she never liked to acknowledge it, the thought of her homeland always brought up unpleasant memories.

Recollections of a fragmented era; a period she preferred to push away; a time synonymous with brokeness; a lost past.

Though everyone knew she was originally from that West African country, no one knew the true circumstances of her departure from there and arrival in South Africa. No one needed to know anything as harrowing and unhappy as her experience, she always told herself.

"Here, that is it", Maria broke through her reverie, extending a short list of names to her.

Taking it, Angelou scanned through it. They were all academic types. Their names written in that unmistakable scribble of Professor Nomvete's.

There was Dr and Mrs Ernest Milton from University of Botswana. Dr Evelyn Hani from Windhoek Institute of Contemporary Arts. Mr Matt De Villiers from John Hopkins in the USA who was on sabbatical at Fort Hare University in the Eastern Cape. Dr Nnanna Kalu from University of Port Harcourt in Nigeria. Lastly, Prof Simon Wakiwunzi from Makerere University in Uganda.

Prof Nomvete liked to "internationalise" the department's week celebrations with such foreign guests and this year was obviously no exception.

"I'm sure you must be looking forward to the Doctor from Nigeria even though you probably don't know him", Maria remarked cheerily.

If only she knew.

Angelou smiled back with a slight nod of the head in apparent agreement with her friend. In truth she didn't know him and hadn't even heard of him, but she wasn't keen on any visitor from her homeland because rather than create a feeling of nostalgic reunion, it only stirred up a replay of depressing events from the past and reminded her of bygone times that were better forgotten.

Whoever this Kalu was from Nigeria, Angelou resolved that the less she had to do with him throughout the celebrations, the better.

But as she got stuck into preparations for the celebration week, the thought of the visitor from Nigeria refused to go away.

Like little drops of dew on an early winter morning.

CHAPTER FIVE

Many waters cannot quench the fire of love

They had met inside NO CONDITION IS PERMANENT.

"Kedu", *he greeted the young woman sitting beside him in the rickety mammy-wagon.*

"Biko...", *he pressed on oblivious of her quizzical look.*

"I'm sorry I don't understand. I'm not Igbo"

"You are not? Oh sorry, I thought you were"

"That's ok, most people think I am"

"So what are you? Or where are you from?"

"I'm from Benin, but we also speak a lot of Yoruba in my place. My parents are from Sabongida-Ora. It is what people call Akoko Edo"

"Oh, ok I've heard a bit about that. So what are you doing in Owerri?"

"I'm a student.. just completed Standard Six. I wrote my Cambridge last week"

"Really?"

"Yes, really. My auntie is a teacher, and I live with her"

"Ok, so do you like Owerri?"

"Very well. It's a big town, not like Sabo where I grew up"

"Umm, but Owerri is not as big as Enugu, or Onitsha where we are coming from, or even Lagos"

"Well for me, it is big. Remember I am from a village"

"So Sabo is a village?"

"Well, it looks so to me. So what did you want to ask me?"

"Oh I was wondering if you could shift a little. I am pressed to the window here"

"Are you serious? Me shift? You are twice my size!"

"Ok, then it has to be that woman beside you with two yam tubers on her chest"

"Don't be rude....can't you see she's not a young woman anymore? Big people also have a right to use public transport"

"Yes I know but so do tiny people like me too"

"Umm, if you say you are tiny, what would someone like me say?"

They continued this kind of small talk up until the wagon, stylishly called 'NO CONDITION...' by most commuters, stopped at Orogwe on the outskirts of Owerri where Chinedum alighted. He promised to come to check her at her auntie's place in Owerri anytime he found himself in the divisional capital soon.

'Soon', turned out to be just four days later. Chinedum had been overwhelmed by the young lady's composure, obvious intelligence, good manners and wit. He couldn't keep his mind off their chance meeting and when the weekend arrived, he told his mother he had some appointment in Owerri and breathlessly boarded 'NO CONDITION' for the two-shilling trip to Owerri.

He easily found the address at old Shell Camp which the lady, Anjolaoluwa, had written on a notepad for him. A very impressive young man himself at 27, Chinedum was still a bachelor due to his demanding tastes. Endless lectures and entreaties by his doting mother to make him bring home a potential bride had yielded nothing. He had no time for the many young ladies in Orogwe, who covered themselves in

23

war-paint, erroneously believing it to be make-up. Worse, most of them lacked proper education and it actually irritated him the way they literally threw themselves at men, especially if such men had a good government job.

Even up at Owerri where he worked, it wasn't very different. Most of the girls preferred to go out with so-called "big-men" who could take them shopping, lavish money on them and buy a bicycle for their mothers. He never believed you had to spend your way into a girl's heart. With or without money, he used to tell his good friend and colleague, Nnanna, "a woman will still dump you if she doesn't feel anything for you. So to avoid losing both ways, it's better you keep your money and let her convince you of her love. If she proves herself, you spoil her. If she's just pretending, she'll soon get tired and go after someone who can spoil her".

Though he longed for a good woman who would be a worthy partner to him, he always told himself that he would know when the right lady crossed his path.

Anjolaoluwa looked like the proverbial fish that would bite that long-dangling bait. He liked the girl.

Native highlife music from local crooner, Kabaka blasted from a turntable out of one of the open windows facing him as he knocked gingerly on the door of Block 15A that she had written down for him.

A tall, well-dressed, middle-aged lady immediately yanked the door open, looking down on Chinedum from the doorway, which was three, short steps from where he stood.

"Yes?"

"Abeg Madam", he responded in the pidgin English common in majority of communities in Southern Nigeria. "Abeg, I dey ask for Anjola"

"Anjie...who told you to come here? Don't you know that girl is too young to be going out with men?

"I'm sorry Ma.... I didn't know"

"Did she ask you to come here? How do you know where she lives? Do you even know how old she is?", question after question tumbled out of the woman's mouth, leaving Chinedum more and more perplexed.

"Em...sorry Ma, No, I don't...Yes, she gave me..sorry, I....", he stammered irrepressibly.

"Sorry Madam", he tried again, "I was just passing by and remembered that she mentioned her address to me last time, so I thought I should just say hello. If it is a problem, I will go now". His apparent lack of confidence surprised even himself, because it was quite unusual with him.

"It is not a problem, young man", the woman replied with a smile. "We are not used to men asking for Anjie, that's why I was curious. Please come in. I sent her across the street, but she'll be back anytime from now".

'Anytime from now' eventually turned out to be almost 30minutes by which time the woman had introduced herself as Anjola's auntie. She seemed to warm up to Chinedum, asking him about himself, his family, his job and trying her best to determine how much he actually knew about Anjola.

Anjola couldn't believe her eyes when she walked-in on return from the errand, to find Auntie Ada sharing jokes with the young man she met on the mammy-wagon days back. She also had thought of him a lot since their chance meeting but had decided to erase him from her mind since the possibility of them meeting again was almost non-existent. She hardly remembered his name and Owerri was full of so many like him in search of innocent, young girls that would fall prey to their wiles. So.....

"Why did it take you so long? I almost sent Emeka to go look for you", Aunt Ada interrupted her thoughts.

"Sorry Aunty...the woman wanted different colours from the one I took, so I waited for her to give me the exact types she wanted"

"Oooh, so she doesn't like it anymore. Dis woman sef!"

"Anyway, you have a visitor who has been dieing to see you", Aunty Ada remarked wth a mischievous grin

"Ah Aunty...how do you know? He doesn't look like someone about to die..ha, ha!"

They often played these kind of games. Her Aunty was a very liberal but firm woman who, since she lost her husband eight years back, had scrapped a living out of her meagre pay from the school. She had two young children of her own but had warmly welcomed Anjola into her home since the girl was 10. Now just having turned 17, she was proud that she had developed under her nose to become a pretty young woman with her head in the right place. The fact that she was an only child – having lost her mother to childbirth and her father remarrying and moving to the Western part of the country – never seemed to matter to her. The skinny, underfed 10year-old she took into her home the very year her own husband exited this world was now like her own flesh and blood.

They both complimented each other incredibly well. Anjola looked after Aunty's little ones, Emeka and Uju, while also doing most of the chores around the house. She woke up at crack of dawn to draw water from the public tap two houses away and kept up the momentum for the rest of the day. She washed, cleaned, scrubbed, bathed the little ones and walked them to school. Her slight frame was very deceptive to the onlooker. For her, every second of the day counted. She never missed a beat.

An excellent cook, Aunty had since ceded control of the kitchen to her expert hands. She organized the house *and the little kids perfectly. Everything was planned and executed around the two-bedroom house like a military operation. Aunty often joked that Anjola was the wife of the house, while she was the husband. But the older woman loved her ward to bits. Even her own children couldn't draw out more love from her than she felt for Anjie – as they all affectionately called her.*

Despite her hectic house chores, Anjie was also as bright as a button at school. Aunty would never forget the day she returned home to find her weeping silently at the backyard. When she sought her out and asked what it was, she tearily showed her the report sheet for the end of term exams, where she came second. Any other child would have gladly accepted being second after a whole term's work. Not Anjie. She coveted the best position in the class and burst her guts to stay there. Her teachers never stopped complimenting her. She mopped up everything they taught in school like a sponge. Her memory was razor-sharp. As a parent, you couldn't wish for a better child.

Aunty managed to tell Chinedum most of these about Anjie that fateful day and as they got to know him better, they accepted him as a part of the family. Aunty liked him, especially when he told them more of himself. How he was also a semi-orphan. How his father died when he was barely one. How his mother refused to remarry because she wanted to devote herself to her only child. How he went through school both in Owerri and Umuahia before completing Cambridge in 1963 and had since been working with a transport company as a Supervisor.

Though she didn't show it initially, Anjie liked him also. His appearance; his confidence; his deep knowledge; his dreams for the future; his tenderness; his patience with her.

He was a fulfillment of the kind of man she had quietly dreamt would come and steal her heart one day. She wasn't a noisy person, but she wasn't shy either. She read a lot. Apart from her school books, she developed a passion for romance literature. She never could have enough of other women's stories and escapades with the opposite sex often from faraway lands. She lived and loved a world where a woman would meet her prince charming, who would woo his prized princess with songs, poetry, unbridled affection and sensitivity. She dreaded a broken heart. Or an unfaithful lover. Though still younger than a lot of the women she read about, she knew what she wanted out of a relationship.

Chinedum also enjoyed reading, but his choice was often limited to works by prominent Igbo writers like Chukwuemeka Ike, Chinua Achebe and Cyprian Ekwensi. Ike's Toads For Supper was a favourite of his, of which he digested the stories over and over with Anjie.

As days turned into months, they grew closer and closer and Anjie saw in Chinedum the epitome of her romantic dreams. He was the apple of her starry eyes, just as he adored every bone in her body. At 17, she had filled-out quite well for a girl her age and her beauty beamed like a beacon.

Things moved frenetically between them. Aunty Ada read the signs early and chipped in regular bits of encouragement. She liked the young man. She also knew Anjie was a special girl with exceptional beauty coupled with grace, who had incredible reserves of tenderness. She knew a girl like her would attract lots of male attention but her extra-sensory gifts and far-sightedness would help her sift out the right man for herself. Of course, she was still quite young but she wasn't in the same league, mentally, with her age mates. She had the brain and brawn of 25year-old and the older woman trusted the younger girl's judgement. So often in their almost *eight-year cohabitation, Anjie had proved her aunt wrong on issues as diverse as cooking, choice of clothes, the little children's health and even money matters.*

She, as they often say in those parts, had an old head on a young shoulder.

CHAPTER SIX

There is no coincidence in the vocabulary of life. All things happen for a reason.

The class finally broke up with a sigh of relief from most of the young men and women who has sat through the 60 minutes of boring monotone.

Basic Statistics was no one's favourite course and so nobody cared to develop any semblance of interest. The lecturer himself didn't help matters with his drab delivery and low-volume voice. Most of the time, no one heard what he was saying. Accordingly, none of his students had much idea of what he was teaching. He never asked questions, apart from the perfunctory "understand?" and never waited for any response before packing his files and exiting.

He was a mechanical kind of man. Very predictable. Not interested in change or variety and had no interest whether his students understood him or not.

His style suited everyone concerned. At the end of every semester, all students passed his course with an average score. In the history of the university, no single student had ever failed Basic Statistics since Mr Simphiwe Tshabalala had been teaching it. He demanded very little from his students and gave even less in return. It was a very convenient arrangement that suited all parties. At the end of every semester, the relationship between students and lecturer always ended amicably with both participants going their different ways. Mutually satisfied.

Even a gifted scholar like Rupert found Tshabalala's lecturer very uninspiring and dull. Such was his relief that chilly afternoon when the class was over and everyone spilled out of the room to varied destinations.

As he headed for the exit, someone tapped him on the shoulder and turning around, he found himself starring into the bespectacled eyes of Tshabalala.

'Yes, Sir?'

"Oh my dear I just wanted someone to accompany me to my office to sort out some of your assignments from last week. You think you can spare some minutes?"

"Of course Sir, with all pleasure", he fell in beside him.

At the office, Rupert saw why Tshabalala chose him. Most of the scripts were marked but not yet recorded into a comprehensive list, which would help the lecturer assess all the students after the end of the semester examinations. Time was clearly against such task as the exams were billed to start in less than three weeks.

The lecturer needed help to fill in the marks and contribute towards computing the students' continuous assessment before the start of exams. Only someone as quick and smart as Rupert could accomplish such task with minimal supervision.

After explaining what he wanted, Tshabalala left him to set about it, making an excuse that he had more work to do in his office.

It was tedious work but three hours later, Rupert had finished with the last scripts. To his surprise, it was already getting dark outside, which was always the case in winter.

Handing over the completed assessments to a snoring Tshabalala, Rupert accepted his mumbled gratitude and proceeded to see himself out.

That was when he bumped into a lady, who was also shutting the office door next to Tshabalala's office.

"Oh sorry Maam, didn't see you"

"That is ok my dear. What's your name again? Ain't you in one of my classes?"

"Yes Maam, its Level 300. I'm Rupert. Rupert Mabizela"

"Oh, yes that's right", she feigned ignorance of him. "I didn't know you came around to the offices so late"

"Oh Maam, I was just helping Mr Tshabalala with some assignments"

"Alright..poor Simphiwe, he sure needs help. Don't we all do?"

Rupert didn't know how to respond this time. The venerable Ms Angelou wasn't the easiest person to hold a conversation with.

She sensed his unease.

"So how do you get home at this late hour?", she enquired

"Oh, em I'll just walk to the second gate where I'll hope to catch those taxis going to Auckland Park. From there, I hope to get another one going to Bree Street, which is just a ten minute walk to my place"

"Sounds like a trip based on a lot of hope, ay?", she retorted with a smile. "Y'know what? Why don't I convert all that hope into reality for you and drop you off at Bree?"

"Oh Maam, you don't have to do that"

"Oh student, I want to do that!"

He smiled at her sense of humour.

She liked his smile. She couldn't believe how well this was all going.

Their meeting by the door hadn't been a coincidence at all. She had heard his voice when he went into the office about three hours back with Tshabalala and had waited patiently for him to come out. When he did at last, she made her move. She was very much surprised by her boldness with a student but her sense of adventure got the better of her intuition.

She, the reverred, bluestockinged Angelou Fanteni.

Quite unbelievable.

CHAPTER SEVEN

When a man loves a woman / He can do no wrong –
Percy Sledge

She did not stop at Bree Street. She insisted she would prefer to take him straight to his residence. Apart from it being an extension of assistance, it was a very calculated ploy to find out where he lived.

Home proved to be a huge block of flats at the corner of Harrison and Commissioner streets. It was very much inner city style and she couldn't believe the amount of noise and bedlam on the streets at that time of the day. She considered how very lucky she and her colleagues were to be cocooned away in the serene surroundings of the campus where the loudest noise was likely to be rustle of leaves on a tree.

During the course of the drive, she found out much more about this mystery man. He was an only child. His parents lived in faraway Kimberley in the Northern Cape. His father, in his words, was a "struggling maize farm manager", who oversaw a plantation owned by some Boer family. He had been at that job for almost twenty years and Rupert spent a good part of his childhood on the plantation.

"So can I call you plantation boy?", Angelou teased him as she navigated the traffic expertly.

34

"No Maam, my friends will wonder where the name came from. I prefer not to let anyone know my background".

"Why? There is nothing there to be ashamed of", she probed.

"It's true but the less they know about me the better, I believe".

"Anyway, you don't seem to have too many friends at school", she suggested carefully.

The remark surprised him and it showed on his face as he regarded her from across the front passenger seat where he sat.

"How did you know that Maam?"

It was her turn to be surprised.

"Em, I take delight in studying my students", she lied.

"So you know all their habits?", he asked boldly

"Not all their habits of course. I just look out for those that seem interesting"

"You mean the ones that interest you?"

He had her in a corner there.

"Em..I just think it is nice to know a bit about some of your students", she replied defensively.

Quickly, she changed the subject. Asking him what his plans for the future were and sundry related topics, as she carefully steered clear of anything personal.

By the time she dropped him off at his place, it was clear to both of them that this looked like the start of something.

Angelou liked him. All her feelings and imaginations about him of the past three-and-something years, appeared to have been right.

He was attractive.

Also very matured and a fine young man. The sort he would have wished for as a son.

But was it as a son she liked him? She wasn't sure about that and preferred to suppress any motherly affections that might be springing into her thoughts.

During their conversation, she had unwittingly let out that she had been observing him. What could that mean to him? How would he take that? He seemed a very private person who avoided close acquaintances.

Had she scared him away? What would he think of her now? Her subtle moves and efforts had finally brought them together but would she dare tempt fate further?

All the time it took her to drive back to her apartment on the campus, and crawl tentatively into bed, her heart never stopped hammering against chest. With excitement.

She was like a teenager falling in love for the first time. Is that what this was? Falling in love?

What would people say? She, a mid-forty year old spinster, involved with this boy? This student who rightly ought to be her child!

In her wildest dreams and craziest imaginations, she never for once thought she could be faced with such dilemma again.

Not again. Not after all those decades since her first love was snatched away mercilessly. Not again. Oh not again.

After endlessly tossing around in bed, Angelou finally fell into a fitful sleep as the long arm of the clock hit 2.00am.

CHAPTER EIGHT

Plantation Boy / C'mon and get going – Boney M.

Angelou tried to avoid 'Plantation Boy' as best as she could over the next days. But it proved a fruitless and half-hearted effort.

He sought her out. Whatever tumult was going on inside her, it was nothing compared to the inferno she had lit in Rupert's heart.

The ease of her manner that night on their way home and her willingness to engage in conversation surprised him. It was directly and completely different from the image and impression everyone had of Miss Angelou. Not only was she friendly, he learnt that night that she was also funny, cordial, jovial and playful. She didn't match up to the stand-offish and aloof figure everyone assumed she was.

The more he thought about their encounter, the more he wanted to know about this strange woman. Why wasn't she married? Why did she live alone? What was her story?

Of course no one could provide answers to such personal questions other than Angelou herself. And there was no point in asking around. Rupert wasn't that sort of person anyway.

So, very much against his character, he summoned up courage four days later, after lunch hour, to knock on her office door.

At first there was silence.

He knocked again and this time, a "come in please" invited him in.

He entered and thankfully, there wasn't anyone else there.

"Oh Maam, I just wanted to come to thank you for your help the other night"

She was seated behind a huge desk covered with all manner of books, papers and files of all shapes and colour. She was also dressed in a smart, black suit which was open at the top revealing a bright, pink shirt underneath.

"Stop it my dear. I didn't do anything too special"

"Well to me, it was special"

"Really? If you say so I believe it. It is nice seeing you again"

"Oh thanks Maam. I just wanted to express my gratitude"

"That is ok. You make it sound like it was a big deal. It was my pleasure really"

"I have been thinking of some way of returning the favour and thought I should come and see you"

'I wonder what you have in mind", Angelou replied with renewed interest.

Standing this close to her now, he realized that she was quite attractive. All the years she had stood there in front of them in class did not do justice to her looks at all.

It was like he was seeing her for the first time.

"I was thinking Maam....I noticed your car needed a wash. So I'm thinking why don't I come to your place and wash it inside out for you?"

Angelou almost couldn't believe her ears. The boy was from another planet.

Could any lecturer imagine or even dream of an undergraduate offering to roll up their sleeves and dirty their hands washing cars for them? Surely not in this day and age of fading moral values.

"You didn't really mean that, did you?", she checked just to be sure she heard right.

"I do mean it Maam"

They argued mildly back and forth for the next ten minutes before Angelou finally succumbed, still not believing her ears.

'I'll let you do it though if you'll also grant me one wish", she negotiated further.

"Ride on Maam", he sang out from where he stood.

"I'll let you wash the car if you'll also let me call you Plantation Boy"

He almost burst out laughing. This woman knew how to get at him.

"Ok, ok, you can", he conceded, grinning from ear to ear. He had not stopped smiling since walking into the office and it was a wrench to now have to leave.

Clearly, he liked talking to her and it seemed she did also.

Still smiling, he excused himself and strolled happily out; pinching himself to make sure that something absolutely unimaginable just days ago, was actually now happening.

CHAPTER NINE

A friend indeed is a shoulder to lean on

Maria didn't know what to say to her friend.

It had been totally unexpected when Angelou called her on the phone, asking her to drop by at her office after close of work. In all their five-year association, she could count the number of times her friend lost her composure either in public or privately.

"Maria please", she pleaded over the phone, "you have to come over after work. I know you told me this morning about the hairdresser's but it can wait, surely"

"Angel, you know how long it took me to get an appointment and..."

"Oh we can always reschedule. I'll drive by her place from here so we'll tell her to give you a new date, ok?"

"Oh Angel", Maria moaned.

"Oh Santa Maria!", she used her pet name, "Thank you, thank you my sweetie"

Apart from her surprise at the different mood of her friend, Marie was equally curious to know what all the excitement was about. She and Angelou lived very predictable lifestyles and they both could say where the other was at almost anytime of the day. Habit was second nature to both of them. Devoid of partners and a social life, they actually spent considerable time in each other's company after work.

When they were not at work, they were either with each other or in their respective beds.

It was that straight forward between them both.

CHAPTER TEN

Those who make peaceful change impossible, make violent change inevitable.

As 1968 approached and everybody got caught up in frenzied anticipation of what the New Year would bring, the two young lovers agreed that they couldn't imagine a future without each other.

"Oh Anjie, Anjie my love......I can't even think of life without you. I can't my dear. Soon as you start at the teacher training college, I will have to go and see Aunty"

"See Aunty for what?"

"You know now"

"Since when did I become a soothsayer? I don't know what is on your mind o!"

"Ok. You'll know after I've spoken to Aunty. I'm sure she'll tell you"

"Aaah, you this youngman. Whatever it is you want to go and see Aunty for, I'm sure isn't important, because if it is, you'll tell me first".

Of course, she had a very good idea what the planned meeting with Aunty was all about but traditional Igbo courtesy demanded that a woman ought not to have fore knowledge of plans to ask for her hand in marriage; at least until her parents or guardian inform her that she was being sought-for by a potential groom. And this would be after the groom's family had visited to register their son's interest.

As elaborate and long-drawn-out as the process was, the young lovers were confident that everything would go according to plan and they would soon be joined together in holy matrimony.

Events over the next few weeks sadly proved them wrong.

It had been threatening throughout the whole of 1967 and every Nigerian was tensed across the length and breadth of the country.

Residents of Owerri, the heart of Igboland were no exception to the pervading mood in the country and actually had more reason than others, to be concerned. Whatever happened between the two major sides would affect the people of this sleepy town as it was very much in the eye of the storm about to engulf all Igbos.

Much earlier that year, January 5 to be precise, the reconciliation talks in Aburi, Ghana had broken down. All entreaties, all through the year to both parties to listen to the voice of reason failed and the drumbeats grew sinisterly louder and melancholic.

The Nigerian military leader, Yakubu Gowon upped the ante considerably on the 5th of May, when he announced the break-up of the erstwhile three regions in the country, into twelve new states. The monolithic Eastern region, which encompassed all Igbo-speaking people as well as several minority tribes was split into three new states. His intention was clear if not overt. He wanted Emeka Ojukwu's Igbo-speaking kinsmen separated from the other minority tribes that lived on the Atlantic ocean seaboard. Thus the Eastern Region now disintegrated into Rivers, South Eastern states, leaving the Igbos isolated and squeezed into only the new East Central State. Of more importance to the calculating Gowon was the intelligence that the riverine, minority tribes were sitting on huge, unexplored reserves of crude oil – a very vital resource that was destined to land Nigeria in the big league of oil exporting nations. Gowon was not prepared to let Ojukwu lay his hands on such precious cargo, which informed his map-redrawing joker.

On the morning of May 30th, Emeka Ojukwu responded.

Bowing to wide support and popular consensus amongst his fellow Igbos, he declared that the whole of old Eastern Region (including of course, Gowon's new riverine states) was ceding from the rest of Nigeria under the new name Republic of Biafra.

It could only mean one thing.

The drumbeats were becoming a cacophony.

War was looming.

It inevitably broke out in the first week of July, 1967 and in that month alone, major Biafran cities of Okrika, the university town Nsukka and Port Harcourt fell to the superior firepower of the Nigerian troops. The loss of Port Harcourt was especially crushing to the Biafran war effort because it denied the young nation crucial access to the sea and supplies from ships of friendly nations.

Allover the Eastern Region especially among the civilians, news of such setbacks were kept away from their ears. Ordinary folk were plied with heroic efforts of Biafran soldiers on the war front – blindfolding them to the reality of their collective fate. In truth, Biafran troops recorded successes, like the stunning foray and capture of Benin City and Ore deep inside Nigerian territory. It however eventually proved to be mere hiccups in a steady Nigerian onslaught.

It was in the midst of this haziness that Chinedum and Anjie were innocently going about their romance and building-up expectations of a happy married life.

That bliss was shattered on the evening of January 6, 1968 when Aunty Ada returned home sad and dejected. She and other teachers in her school had been informed by the Headmaster that the school was going on impromptu holidays – just two days after they resumed for a new term. The headmaster gave no particular reason except to say it was in support of the war effort.

However rumours were rife that the school and all others in and around Owerri were being evacuated in readiness for use by the Biafran High Command. Even more vicious rumours had it that Enugu, the seat of the Biafran government had fallen into the hands of advancing Nigerian soldiers and in a mad scramble, government workers, soldiers, civilians had fled the city and scattered into neighbouring towns. It was even said that the seat of government had since relocated to Umuahia and that Owerri would also be sharing the burden.

Most people preferred not to believe such stories.

So fervent and fierce was the blind patriotism with which all Igbos welcomed both their new nation and the bitter war being fought to defend it, that the thought of defeat at the end of the road was unthinkable.

But Aunty Ada was greatly disturbed.

For months throughout the last year, she had seen more and more of her male colleagues disappear from the classrooms. If she or any other female teacher asked questions, they were given the standard reply – indisposed. A school boasting over 40 teachers, soon had just 12 left – all of them female. The bemused women had been forced to take on more pupils from the other classes. Even though everyone knew there were clashes between Biafran and Nigerian soldiers in faraway places like Abakaliki, Nsukka and Calabar, none of them dare openly suggest that it was a full-scale war that had forced their male colleagues into conscripts.

But now, the school along with all others in the town were shutting down.

"My dear Anjie", she started gravely as the tune of martial music – now increasingly regular from the omnipresent Radio Biafra – floated around the small sitting-room.

"My dear, I have had to stop work. We are not told exactly why. They said they'll communicate to us. How, we don't know".

"Don't worry Aunty, they will soon call you back"

"My child, I don't know when that will be o. How do we cope? We have not been paid for two months now. Nobody knows what is happening anymore"

Anjie didn't know how to lift her aunt's spirits because she too had heard rumours that all students at the teacher training college she attended in town would soon be asked to report for compulsory military training.

A few of the boys had even stopped coming altogether and there were suggestions they had gone to 'support' the "clashes" – as Radio Biafra liked to call what was happening elsewhere.

The gathering clouds enveloping the entire Biafran nation came filled with uncertainty, fear and destruction. Despite what the government propaganda machinery was feeding its citizens, people were dieing in their thousands both from the bullets of superior Nigerian firepower and hunger.

Unknown to the simplefolk in places like Owerri, death was at the door. Several towns and cities had truly fallen to the advancing enemy forces. More and more soldiers were surrendering daily and the war was becoming a bloody and regretful walkover. Ojukwu's rhetorics were not living up to the test of gallantry on the battlefield.

But as 1968 dawned on their lives, very few Igbos understood the situation and their place in the new nation, Biafra. Chinedum and his lover fell very much within this blanket of ignorance. Like millions of other unsuspecting Igbos, they were all being blindfolded in a huge cloak of delusion and deceit.

CHAPTER ELEVEN

A problem shared is a problem half solved

"So have you got the appointment?"

"What appointment?"

"Oh com'on, you know now. Everyone knows you'll be the next HOD. I'm sure that is what you called me to discuss", Maria was certain.

"You unbelievable woman, what will I do without you?" Angelou remarked, rolling her dark eyes.

Frowning, Maria threw up her hands.

"So what was all the excitement about? It had better be worth it 'cos I had to cancel with the hairdresser for it".

Angelou smile, taking her time to dwell more on what she was about to tell her beloved friend.

"Com'on what is it? You didn't make me come down here just to admire you, right?" she asked in mock exasperation.

They were at their favourite meeting place; the coffee lounge inside the Gordart gallery at the middle class neighbourhood of Melville. It was across the road from the sprawling campus and they liked it because it took them away from the devout seriousness of the school surroundings. Also, there was the slim chance of being bumped into by colleagues and students.

"Ok, ok my dear", she lowered her voice, looking round the tiny café. "This is it", she paused again looking into Maria's blue eyes. "I think I'm in love"

"You are what? You? Angelou? Who? What? Angel?", Maria blurted senselessly.

"Calm down, calm down Maria", Angelou grabbed her friend's hands, while keeping their eyes locked together.

"Oh my goodness Angel, what is going on with you? Ok, come to think of it I must have been as blind as a bat not to notice anything"

"Com'on Maria, it is not that obvious"

Maria still stared at her friend with horror written allover her face. She just couldn't get her head round it. How could a 45year-old, never-married-woman suddenly fall in love? Could it be a joke? Was Angelou pulling her leg or something?

"Hello? Wake up", Angelou slapped her friend's thighs playfully. 'You look like you've just seen a ghost"

"Yes Angel, I sure do feel like I've seen one. It's like me hearing that my 84 year-old grannie is pregnant. Next thing I know, pigs would start flying!".

"Com'on it's not so hair-raising", Angelou croaked, struggling to find the nerve to go into the details of her big secret.

"You haven't even asked me who the guy is?", she reminded Maria.

"Ok, yeah, sure who is the lucky bloke?"

"I bet that would be the bigger shock", Angelou promised.

"Umm, don't know about that"

"Ok for crying out loud, it's Rupert Mabizela".

"Who? Where does he teach?"

"You don't know Rupert? The boy in Level...."

"What?!", Maria couldn't believe her ears. Now this was truly huge.

"You mean the guy in Part three who is top of the class?", Maria's blue eyes widened as saucers. "Oh my God, Angel, tell me this is some kind of joke. You surely can't be..."

"Yes, Maria, I'm serious", she cut her short, smiling." I like him".

"Angelou!", she cried using her full name, "Are you sure about this? How long has it been going on? What will people say? Don't you think he's too young? What..?"

Angelou cut in again to dampen the wave of fear engulfing her friend "It's ok Maria. We've been seeing each other for weeks now. I didn't want to tell you anything until I was a hundred percent sure about him. It's a big decision for me as well but I like him. He's not a boy actually. He's going to be 30 this November and very matured and wise. You'll like him too. Oh Maria, he sweeps me away all the time. I know it's strange and crazy and I'm old enough to be his mother, but I know in my heart I want to be with this man, Maria. Please, please...!"

"Oh Angel, what has come over you?"

"Maria please", she moved closer to the white woman, gathering her in her arms as they hugged each other severely

"What do you mean, 'please'?", Maria mumbled, wrapping her arms round her friend too.

"I mean please understand. I know it is hard but I need you to understand my reasons and accept it. I need you Maria. We've been through so much together. I never planned for this, you know. I wasn't looking for anyone. We always said we'll both be there for each other. That we'll both stand by each other. Remember how you vowed never to be with another man after Gary. How I respected your decision even after Gary kept on writing and writing and trying to arrange a visit."

She stopped for breath and then ploughed on again.

"Oh Maria it's been tough. Very tough but we've been there for each other. You made me strong also. You filled my empty life. You helped me overcome all the pain and loneliness. I couldn't have coped all these years without you. I know I couldn't. I drew strength from you. I got inspiration from your determination. I leaned on you. I still want to lean on you Maria. Please, please help me Maria!".

"It's ok Angel. It's ok", the older woman fondly patted her friend's head hanging over her shoulder. Unconsciously they were both weeping silently, hanging onto each other like sisters. Except of course, one was white and the other black.

"It's ok Angel", Maria repeated. Despite the shock of the revelation, she had to accept her friend's decision and back her. It was the least she could do.

Yes, the boy was young and still not independent enough to engage a woman of Angelou's age and stature in a relationship, but well, it wasn't the end of the world.

An age gap of fifteen years was big but not impossible to bridge if two people were mature and loving enough.

She trusted Angelou. She knew she wouldn't have succumbed so easily after all these years. She wasn't a person who acted on impulse. She must have thought everything through with a clear head. She knew her well enough. She wasn't desperate either, she was sure of that. After all, since she had known her, she had known of a couple of men who had flirted seriously with her, hoping she would respond to their advances. There was that scientist from Vaal Technikon in Vereeniging who they met at a seminar three years ago. He was nice, well-dressed and still good-looking even at 50 but Angelou never blinked in his direction.

There was also the coloured doctor from the Chris Hani Baragwanath. What was his name again? Coetzer or Courtney or Cusack. She wasn't sure anymore. He had sent several flowers, followed by endless phonecalls to the receptionist downstairs, asking for Angelou. He even once drove to the school in an attempt to surprise her, inviting her out for dinner but Angelou never budged.

Maria knew her friend, even though well in her 40s, was still very attractive. Having never had a child, she had been lucky to maintain her figure. Blessed with long, slim legs; a slim, taut waist; wrapped inside curvaceous hips, Angelou could easily pass for a thirty year-old. She exercised almost daily, walked at every opportunity to stay fit and ate sensibly. Not for her were junk stuff like sugar, fast food or alcohol. She always maintained a healthy diet packed with vegetables and fruits. Her breasts were still firm and inviting. Her eyesight still as sharp as a hawk's. Most women her age envied her and coupled with her ever-rising profile, her star shone as bright as day. She was a true icon; head and shoulders above most of her peers in brains and beauty. All these considered, it had always been a big mystery why she had remained single when most men would have given an arm to be seen with her.

The sound of Angelou sniffing on her shoulder stirred her back into the present.

"It's ok Angel. Really it's ok. You know I'll always be there for you, baby"

"Thanks Maria. You are my saint truly", she hugged her closer. It was like a huge burden had been lifted off her shoulders.

"Hey!", Maria raised her head to look into her friend's wet eyes. "Hey, I say go for it girl. Go for it. Who cares if you are 50 and he's 30? Why waste away with an old witch like me? Go for it baby!"

Her words drew a relieved smile from Angelou. It was very much typical of Maria to make light of every situation.

Oh, what would she do without her? Her Santa Maria.

CHAPTER TWELVE

Cometh the hour, cometh the man

The hall was aglow with blazing lights.

Candles atop the several tables added to the illumination, while Kool and the Gang's *Celebration Time* filtered through from small Sony speakers in the background.

Everything had gone according to plan up till this final night.

Sitting in the backroom, staring into the oval mirror on the wall as she touched up her hair, Angelou was relieved to see that all the planning and sleepless nights of the past months had not been in vain.

The Dramatic Arts week was climaxing tonight with the dinner and awards ceremony.

It had been hectic but it filled her with satisfaction that she and her team had delivered a well-organised week of activities.

For the past six days, there had been dances from various student groups; poetry recitals; songs; stage plays; film shows; fashion parades; quiz competitions and for the first time, a karaoke contest among staff members. It was all culminating this night with the awards dinner. The icing on the cake.

The hall was taken up with tables sitting eight people each. Each table was bedecked with white, chiffon material while all the cutlery were shiny silver. Everything had been handled by the caterers recommended to her by a lecturer friend in the Economics department. She was glad she took her advice, because the caterers had not let her down at all.

Celebrate good times, come on! (Let's celebrate)/
Celebrate good times, come on!

There's a party goin' on right here/
A celebration to last throughout the years.

"Ok, that should be enough", Vivian, another female colleague swooned into the room and clasped big, Boer palms around Angelou's shoulders. "They are here now and we should be receiving them. Maria and Prof Nomvete have been asking for you".

Smiling and jumping to her feet, Angelou allowed big Vivian to pull her from the seat, through the small room into the main hall.

All the tables, 25 of them, each with six adjoining seats, had been taken up now. There was a steady gaggle of noise, chatter, laughter, backslaps and handshakes as students, lecturers, invited guests, artistes and visitors all mingled and interacted freely. Everyone seemed to know the other person. So many of the women looked overdressed to Angelou. No that it was any business of hers anyway, but she always wondered why every woman thought she was in some kind of competition with the next female at occasions like this. If not for the formality of the event, she had earlier told Maria, she would have loved to turn up in her trusty jeans and sports jersey. For her, clothes held very little importance in daily life.

Then she spotted him. He was bowing and shaking hands at the same time. He must be talking to someone quite important whom Angelou couldn't see. She immediately tried to avert her eyes, when he also suddenly turned and met her gaze.

She stood transfixed to the spot.

Caught in his spotlight, she looked and felt like a rabbit surprised by headlights. Suddenly, she started sweating slightly.

"C'mon Angel, we have to go receive the VIPs. They are at the door already", Big Vivian appeared again to nudge her into life.

And truly, the entrance was buzzing with all manner of guests and well-dressed invitees announcing their presence.

With Big V acting as a chaperon of sorts, Angelou joined the welcoming party at the door to receive groups of important invitees, who were mostly from outside the country.

After the usual pleasantries and cheek-touching, they were all escorted to the high table, placed a few meters apart from the rest.

A brief prayer was conducted by a celestial-looking man with lots of grey hair, signaling the start of the night which duly commenced with pomp.

So bring your good times, and your laughter too/
We gonna celebrate your party with you.

Whoever chose the song for tonight's event, thought Angelou, deserved an award of their own. She had always liked Kool and the Gang's lyrics and never could chose which one of the brothers, Robert and Ronald Bell's voices was his favourite. She wished she could detach herself from all the excitement around and....

"Hello Angelou, meet Dr Nnanna Kalu one of our invited guests from Nigeria. He is the Deputy Dean of Faculty of Arts from University of Port Harcourt and we have been friends for a long time"

Angelou rose from her seat to accept the extended hands of a strappling, grizzly man who stood rigidly by her chair. He was being introduced by Prof Nomvete, who had not stopped for a minute since the night started. He looked pleased and delighted with the occasion and the whole atmosphere seemed to have put a new spring in his 69year-old body.

"Nice to meet you Sir", Angelou heard a voice that seemed to be coming out of her mouth. What was the matter with her tonight?

If they noticed anything, both men didn't show it as Dr Kalu exchanged more pleasantries with Angelou before moving around the tables to greet other people.

For someone in his capacity occupying such a top post in a university, he seemed quite young. Angelou guessed he couldn't be more than 6-7years older than herself, but he looked ages younger than Prof. Nomvete who was now approaching the mandatory retirement age of 70. Still as HOD. They must be fast tracking lecturers over there in Nigeria, she mused.

Ah Nigeria!

The thought of all those bygone memories came back to her again. She really did not know whether to be sad; or happy; or bitter; or thrilled; or angry; or relieved.

Memories of that country always conjured mixed emotions inside her. What would her life had become if she had remained behind? What would she have been now? Would she have been happier? Or sunken in despair? What would have happened to her dreams and aspirations? Much more poignantly, would she have discovered the one missing thing in her life? The experience of being married and raising children? Would she? Had her departure and flight forever robbed her of that chance to savour motherhood like most women? Would things have been different if she had stayed?

> *We're gonna have a good time tonight*
> *Let's celebrate, it's all right*

Could she really say her life had been a celebration? Celebration of what? Eternal spinsterhood?

'Excuse me Maam", someone tapped her on the shoulder

"Uh? Yes?", Angelou reacted as if caught red-handed. The food in front of her was still untouched. She looked up into the face of her intruder. A young man she often saw around the offices.

"Yes?", she answered again, a bit irritably.

"Professsor Nomvete asked me to request your presence to join him on the high table. He is preparing to give his vote of thanks".

Vote of thanks already? Had the night progressed so far? She glanced at her silver wristwatch and to her absolute shock, she realized that the allotted two hours was almost up.

Without replying, she gathered her shiny, YSL purse and followed the young man to the high table.

By the time they got there, Prof Nomvete had already started his speech.

She sneaked into a chair beside him and without breaking speed, he continued his impromptu address, with a slight nod at her.

He spoke mostly about the achievements recorded in the department throughout his eight years at the helm. He wasn't known as a man of too many words, but tonight, he seemed transformed.

He spoke fluently and authoritatively, reminding everyone of his impending retirement. The light-heartedness of the occasion soon somehow turned into a somber atmosphere as Prof Nomvete consistently repeated the fact this was to be his final appearance at the awards night, in the capacity of HOD.

He thanked everyone for their contribution to what he described as the "family atmosphere" that had existed between staff and students throughout his tenure.

Several rounds of applause and encore greeted almost every sentence of his. Each time he mentioned the name of a lecturer or student, he drew acclaim and loud ovation from the audience.

"Finally, before I come to the end of my speech", he looked up again glowingly, "please permit me to introduce to you the new HOD of the Dramatics Arts department".

A great hush fell on the entire audience as if some mysterious, unseen presence had entered the room.

Professor Nomvete sensed it and milked the occasion to the fullest.

"Let me say briefly that the choice of the new HOD wasn't an easy one to make. All the members of the faculty board argued and disagreed over the names on the shortlist, but after it was put to vote and the final name emerged, everyone agreed that it was a choice well made", he revealed with his usual, infectious smile.

No one however was smiling with him. Anticipation, mixed with tension was thick in the air. But Professsor Nomvete felt infinite pleasure that the hour had finally come for him to do the deed.

"So ladies and gentlemen, please put your hands together for the new HOD of Dramatic Arts..."

"....Dr Angelou Fanteni!"

Feverish clapping. Dragging of chairs. Applause. Hooting. Shouting all erupted at the same time. An incredible din overtook the entire hall, where just seconds earlier there had been graveyard silence.

Celebrate good times, come on!
Celebrate good times, come on!

From her seat, Angelou looked on completely dumbfounded as hands reached out to pull her to her feet. Her lips, rimmed with translucent lipstick, remained open in awe and horror at what was happening around her. No, it couldn't be true.

Come on and celebrate, good times, tonight
'Cause everything's gonna be all right

As she found herself sucked more and more into a growing circle of excited people; all of them descending on her with shouts of 'congratulations! congratulations!', Angelou couldn't resist smiling quietly to herself with the gradual realization that actually, the Bell brothers had been right all along.

There surely was celebration in the air now.

Despite the smiling faces surrounding her, she still sought desperately for him; stretching and craning her neck in a determined attempt to locate him with her eyes. Since that moment earlier in the evening when their eyes had locked together, events had moved too fast for her to seek him out again. But she wanted to see him now. She was certain he was still in the room.

"Whaooooo Angel!", a very familiar voice screamed from behind her.

Even before she turned to acknowledge it, she knew definitely who it was.

Nonetheless, the new HOD managed to disentangle her hands from the several, anonymous human tentacles holding them. Only for her to turn around and find herself wrapped in a heaving, warm, bear hug from an onrushing Maria.

Celebration! Celebration!! Celebration!!!

CHAPTER THIRTEEN

In life, all things have their place and their time

"A man was taken to hospital after sustaining two broken legs. When the doctor asked him how come he broke both legs, he replied, 'I smashed the window of a stereo shop using a manhole cover from the sidewalk in front of the store. As I moved away from the window to see if anyone was watching, I fell down the manhole!'.

A loud peal of laughter ripped through the classroom. Some in the class who couldn't contain themselves anymore were spilling out onto the corridor, in raptures of hilarity.

Napoleon, the cause of the whole uproar sat placidly at the back row with a comical smile on his face.

"Napo ...you are too much!!", someone roared above all the laughter and table-banging.

If he had heard, he didn't give any indication. He just continued smiling.

They were all waiting for the lecturer that took them in Syntax of English 407. It was the first day of lectures in the new semester and after the usual three weeks of registration and accreditation formalities, the real business of learning was about to start across the campus.

For this particular group, this was the start of their final year in a four-year undergraduate programme and this first day of class had a lot of poignant interpretations.

"Ok", Napoleon spoke up again. Everyone fell silent, eager to hear the next joke from his inexhaustible reservoir.

"A man once told his wife that her bum was so big, it looked like a braai stand".

Another round of screams and laughter broke out.

"Ok, ok, that's not the joke. Hold on", Napoleon persisted. "At night one day, the man woke up his wife asking to make love. The woman refused, telling him that, 'Do you expect me to light my braai stand for your small sausage?'

The huge noise that accompanied this story was deafening.

Everyone in the class was in fits and hysterics. More table-banging, clapping, shouting, ear-rending howls filled the air. It was the highest form of commotion imaginable.

Amidst the riotous scene, the new HOD walked in. Aghast.

Gradually, after what seemed like an eternity, sanity returned gradually.

At first, no one noticed her presence. So consumed was everyone with their reaction to Napoleon's funny story that all sense of decorum was lost.

Angelou stood at the door of class; impassive.

The first person to notice her presence was a female student. She pinched the gyrating boy next to her, pointing his attention towards the door and gradually, more and more pairs of eyes turned towards the door and the static, patient figure of the HOD.

Finally, the din in the room subsided as they all acknowledged the presence of Angelou by the door.

"That is what I call immature behaviour", she spoke up at last.

"I heard the noise coming from here, right from my office and thought there was a fight or something. I was even convinced it must be from one of the junior classes. It was a shock to me to find out that it is you finalists that are disturbing everyone's peace", her voice never losing its deliberate calm.

"I hope you all realise this is a breach of the trust I had in you all. I am very disappointed with this sort of behaviour and will expect an apology from everyone of you. I don't intend us to start this new session on a wrong footing because like it or not, we both need each other to succeed here".

"I will not tell you what action I will take now, but I want all your names sent up to me. I will expect one of your representative to bring that list to me before the end of the day in my office."

She turned to leave the room, but on a second thought, she stopped and walked back again.

"Napoleon, we all know how talented you are. Keep it up. I also enjoy laughing, but there is always a time and a place for everything.Most people look up and admire the stars. A champion climbs a mountain and grabs one. I expect you to one day be a champ".

"Meanwhile", she continued with Napoleon, "let me see if you know all the jokes. Try answering this riddle. Ready? Ok. What are the two things you can never have for breakfast?"

Napoleon stood transfixed, but with a slight frown across his brow. The hunter looked very much like the hunted now.

"Yes, Napoleon, I'm waiting", the HOD sang out.

Still no response.

Every other person in the room was amused by this sudden change of tactics. None of them knew their HOD had her own repertoire of riddles.

"Isn't it pap?", Napoleon ventured tentatively.

A couple of the students let out short, sharp giggles, suggesting how ridiculous Napoleon's answer was.

"No way my dear", the HOD responded. "Anyway, I said two things, not one. Ok, I haven't got all day. The answers are lunch and dinner".

A knowing murmur spread through the room.

"I will be expecting the list before the close of the day. Thank you all".

She walked out with a low grumble trailing her exit.

Throughout her tirade, she had not lost her composure and that had made all the students in the room more contrite with guilt. Though her riddle had eased the tension among them, they still felt they had let themselves down in the first place.

Quietly, a sheet was produced and names were scribbled noiselessly one after the other. At a time like this, when the session was starting, no one wanted to be in the bad books of the HOD. Especially an HOD who commanded so much respect and reverence among staff and students alike.

After the compilation of the names, someone suggested that the bearer of the list to the HOD ought to be someone who could appeal to her sense of forgiveness. They argued this point back and forth and eventually agreed that it actually made sense

Relieved at the adoption of the idea, the mover of the motion offered to take the list to the HOD. Himself.

CHAPTER FOURTEEN

True love has a heart of its own

Knock, knock.

She moved lazily towards the door and since the latch wasn't on, she yanked it open quite easily.

Since her elevation to HOD last month, she had resisted a subtle pressure to move from the house to the more swanky accommodation reserved for her new status.

She liked this house. It was average in size and modest enough in accordance with her personal tastes. She had lived in it for the past six years and knew all the peculiar sounds and foibles associated with it. She knew every acre of the two-bedroom building since she moved into it in 1994. The fact that she lived alone even accentuated every detail of the house in her head. Every little bit about the house was ingrained in her subconscious and she liked it that way.

She had decorated every room in the house to her particular passion. All the rooms were covered in pink wallpaper. There was also deliberate attempts to invite nature in with several huge earthenware flowerpots sitting in most corners of the house. She liked the balance between modern, technological gadgets and unspoiled natural world.

Apart from Maria and occasionally, Big V, no one hardly ever came here as she jealously kept her official and private lives apart.

So it was one of them she was expecting to see at the door when she opened it that late evening.

"Oh, its you, how..?"

"I'm sorry Maam. We had one lecture after the other throughout the day, so by the time we got to your office, you had gone out".

"So you felt my place would be a better place to bring the list to?", she asked slyly, boring her eyes into his.

Since their initial contact, they had managed to meet in secret without attracting any attention. Angelou hoped at least no one had noticed anything untoward between her and this young man. She really liked him and though had never told him so, she could see that he enjoyed her company as well.

After coming to wash her car about two months back, he had visited her house again twice and had actually met Maria there once. Angelou had introduced them, though they both knew each other. At least now that something was brewing between them, she told Maria later, she had to be sure that her best friend wasn't left to imagine things herself. Angelou trusted Maria to keep their secrets, secret. At least for the moment.

"Here is the list Maam", he extended a brown A4 size paper towards her with a compilation of all his classmates' names on it.

"I'm sure you did not come all this way to drop a list and then go back. Would it be too much to ask you to come in for a cup of tea?".

Rupert pretended to actually want to go back immediately. But the nerve to say anything in that wise failed him. Isn't this the chance he had been dreaming of for a long, long time? Already mere standing close to her was a moment in wonderland.

"Ok, Maam, thanks", he shuffled inside as she opened the door wider to allow him inside.

A bit unsteady herself, Angelou wasn't sure how to handle this. She felt a strong stirring inside of her. Something akin to a volcano building up. Gathering pace towards an almighty eruption. She suspected what it was and hoped that they would both be able to control themselves. Really?

She dreaded very much also that her will power might fail her.

She wanted him. She wanted him desperately. More than she had ever wanted any member of the male specie in a long, long time. Looking at him now, sitting gingerly on her comfortable cream sofa stoked the fires of intense passion within her fiercely.

He averted his eyes. Leafing through a journal he found by the stool, he couldn't bring himself to make the first move. Whatever that move was.

"What can I get for you Rupert?", Angelou found her voice at last.

He looked up with make-believe surprise on his face.

"Anything Maam. I still hope you have those cream doughnuts you gave me the last time".

"Aha, so you have a sweet tooth also. Ok, I'll get some. I've also got some frozen chicken nuggets. Can you get them out of the fridge and heat them in micro. I'll get the tea stuff from the kitchen".

He rose thankfully to his feet and approached the fridge. Of course, he was no stranger to the house but on this occasion, he felt an ominous storm which was threatening to break out in a way they both would like to happen. He felt something thick and expectant hanging around them both.

The tastily-furnished loungeroom was in semi-darkness, save for a shaft of light streaming in from the streetlamp outside. Soft, rhythm and blue tunes which clearly belonged to Randy Crawford filtered from inside her bedroom. He knew it was her bedroom because she went in and out of it several times the last time he was here.

They both soon brought all the victuals together and a dinner was set on the mahogany dining table.

"So why did they give you the list to bring to me?", she asked out of curiosity.

"Oh they didn't. I actually volunteered to do it because I suggested that someone who could plead with you should be the bearer", he replied in between a bout of nervous lip-chewing.

"So you think you have some power of persuasion over me?", she looked at him directly.

"Of course I don't but everyone knows how strict you are and when you came and reprimanded us this morning, we were worried that we had gone into your bad books"

"Ok, so you all think I'm some kind of witch everyone has to tiptoe around to avoid incurring her wrath"

"Ah Maam, no one thinks you are a witch. We just didn't not want you to think the worst of us, so we thought someone who could talk you out of your anger would help"

"I wasn't angry, was I?"

"Well, you know with you, nobody can be too sure about that"

"What about you? You are supposed to know me better than the rest", Angelou asked testily, her hand shaking slightly as she applied Rama butter to a slice of raisin toast.

They were standing side by side and as he reached out to scoop some sugar with the teaspoon, his hand accidentally brushed her chest, sending sparks of fire through her body. Her nipples, erect and at attention underneath her flimsy coat, throbbed like a radio antenna.

"Oh I'm sorry", he croaked embarrassingly.

Her response was automatic and very unexpected. Her animated body giving her unusual effrontery.

She grabbed his hand and clasped her fingers in it, boring her eyes deep, deep into his. Whatever it was that overcame her, she would never know but what she knew was that she wanted this man. Badly. Now.

"Oh Rupert, Rupert hold me. Please hold me".

He responded as if in a trance. Unsure of how to cope with this strangest of situations, he managed to pull her close to himself. Her rich, jet black hair barely reaching up to his chest.

Her grip was fierce and vice-like. She wasn't prepared to let go of him and it told in her strong, clasped arms around his broad shoulders.

The room appeared to be swimming around in Rupert's head. He wasn't sure anymore where he was or what he was doing here. He only knew that deep in his consciousness, a woman was hanging onto him in the throes of a fierce passion. A woman he adored and admired and had fantasized about for so long.

Hoverin' by my suitcase, tryin' to find a /
Warm place to spend the night

His brain was filled with too many thoughts. Too numerous and convoluted to make any meaning at the moment.

Angelou's twittering body was now wrapped all over him and he enjoyed the breathtaking sensation that it generated inside of him. He had never felt anything like this before. All his previous romantic escapades never prepared him for what he was now experiencing with this woman.

The uneaten dinner on the table was forgotten.

In a flash, their lips locked together. Millions and millions of small bombs exploded all at the same time in his brain. Igniting billions of other fuses in his nervous system. Rendering him unconscious while still on his feet.

High voltage electric currents surged between both their bodies, turning them both into human transformers. Two pairs of hands moved feverishly and excitedly and restlessly over torsos, chests and faces. "That is sooooo good, plantation boy", she managed to mumble several minutes later when she had pulled away from him. Still holding hands, they sat curled up together on the sofa. Unsure of what next to do. Surprised by the unfolding expressions of their mutual desires.

The violence of their intense kiss had knocked a lot of breathe out of them both.

I hear your voice callin' "It's all right."
A rainy night in Georgia,
It seems like it's rainin' all over the world

Outside the house, darkness had descended.

Not a thing moved as both lovers lay entwined in each other's arms; breathing into each other's face; relishing a shared experience that was taking them to wild heights and unbelievable peaks of pleasure as they held hands.

In her heart, she knew now that there was no turning back anymore.

No turning back from him. Her life was never again going back to the lonely path she had known it to be on, for the past three decades.

Oh, have you ever been lonely, people?
And you feel that it was rainin' all over this man's world
You're talking 'bout rainin', rainin', rainin', rainin',

The list of names he had brought lay unattended to by the floor. Completely forgotten in the bliss of the moment.

CHAPTER FIFTEEN

'Brother of love, I have heard that the soldiers are two moons away / They come with many guns and death is waiting for a stranger such as you' – Boney M.

Truth of the matter was Aunt Ada had been relieved of her teacher job along with all the other teachers. There was simply no job anymore; no pupils, no school to return to. Wild rumours of advancing Nigerian soldiers spread like a bushfire in harmattan.

Everywhere there was very little to cheer people up. Markets, shops and shelves were slowly but gradually drying up of essential household items. Where they could be found, their prices went through the roof. Life, as described by a famous West Indian writer was truly becoming "short, nasty and brutish".

It was this gloomy state of affairs that prevailed when Chinedum broached the one subject very dear to his heart, with Nne, his mother. Though they had both discussed his growing interest in 'that Yoruba girl', Nne secretly hoped that the interest would not grow wings and feather his heart's nest.

That early morning, her worst fears were confirmed as her only child roused her from a troubled sleep, seeking to talk. The huge house was silent but her heart pounded inside her chest as if warning her of something ominous.

"Nne, yes I wanted to tell you that", he paused for effect, "that I want to marry her"

'Marry who?', she pretended not to understand clearly.

"Come on Nne, who else could I mean? Anjie of course"

The aging but agile woman yawned, clearing the cobwebs of sleep from her eyes.

"Oh ok, you mean the Yoruba girl".

"Nne, I said stop calling her that. It is not nice especially since you've known her name for over a year now and she'll soon be your daughter in-law"

"But that doesn't mean she has stopped being a Yoruba"

"I know, but it is not her name....anyway Nne, you heard what I said. I want her to be my wife and we need your consent".

Nne's head slumped briefly, before raising it again and looked at his son in the dim, early morning light. A very deep, dull booming noise could be heard very faraway. Like a great thing falling to earth from the sky. No one knew what was going on these days with all manner of stories about fighting in many towns. Just last night, a small group of women and children walked into Orogwe with their belongings on their head. They all looked hungry and tattered. Snatches of information gleaned from them revealed they had come all the way from Okigwe, which was a good 80kms from here.

They said soldiers were coming, but were not sure which side the soldiers were on.

These were really disturbing times. All Ojukwu and his lofty dreams had brought them was scarcity, high prices, fear and women with children from faraway places.

"My son, you can't marry that girl".

Chinedum thought he didn't hear her correctly.

"You mean she won't agree to marry me? No Nne, she has. She is very happy and even says her auntie said she will give us her blessing. Oh, that is no problem Nne, we have....."

"My son", Nne cut him short again, this time with a cheerless finality in her voice. "You didn't hear me well. I said you cannot marry Anjie as you call her".

This could not be happening.

"But Nne, did you not tell me that you were praying to God for a wife for me? Why will you now prevent your own prayers from being answered?".

"I prayed for a wife for you and still do. But not for a wife like your Anjie"

"What is wrong with Anjie, Nne?", he asked apprehensively.

In response, Nne sighed very deeply, drawing her wrapper closer to her body to keep warm.

"Nne, please talk, I say what is wrong with Anjie?", Chinedum frantically asked his mother who looked to have aged all of a sudden.

"My son, I haven't told you why I never remarried after the death of your father.

It was not my wish. You see, they killed your father".

"Who? They? Who?...Nne, what are you saying? Do you mean...?"

"Wait my son, please hear me out, I plead with you. They killed your father. He was a great man and very kind and we were in love just like you are now with the Yoruba girl. But his family were full of wicked people. The people of this village...his people. Because he was rich and successful, they wanted him to marry from amongst them. They tried their best to make him change his mind about me, but he refused. I'm proud of your father my son. They said I was stranger... efulefu they used to call me. That it was a taboo in their *custom for the first son of any family to marry a stranger. I am from Oraifite, you know, after the river... Otamiri River".*

Tears welled up inside of her and dribbled steadily down her face as she spoke. Chinedum sat dumbfounded.

"From the day he brought me home here, he knew no peace. I was scorned and rejected. After 11months of our marriage, he mysteriously fell ill. I spent all the money we had to heal him. He even told me to sell off his two mammy-wagons that went from here all the way to Onitsha. The sickness took all we had but I was not ready to give up on him. He was everything I had. He was my life. Sadly it was all in vain. He finally died one early morning in December in this very room. It was before the Christmas of 1941. You were just ten months old then and I was left looking after both of you".

"None of his family cared to help. Anytime I was asked about his condition, it was only when they came here to ask for money. You see he helped a lot of them while he was strong and even sent some of his brothers' children to school. When he fell sick, they were not interested in his condition and only came here to find out if he made any provision for their children. They called me names and when he died, they accused me of killing him. How could I? They refused to support me in all the burial plans. Only his brother who sells clothes at Aba assisted me. You know him...your Uncle Dike. He did a lot. Him and his wife stood by me throughout my hardship. His wife also, Chinyere isn't from here, so she understood all my tribulations. Luckily for her, they don't live here, so no one could worry her like they did to me. Oh my son, your father's death robbed me of joy in my marriage".

"Why did you never tell me all this Nne?"

"I didn't want you to grow up hating any of them. They are still your family so making enemies with them will not help. My son, after your father's death, they made me swear that I'll not marry again. Not only that, they made me swear that none of my male children will marry outside this village. Luckily or otherwise Chim gave me only you. They made me swear that my children will never bring foreigners into their land through marriage. If they do, then the punishment will be that I'll die mysteriously! Just like your father died"

Chinedum sat still as if struck by lightning. He couldn't believe his ears. Surely all what he just heard couldn't possibly have happened. Surely, an oath or whatever Nne swore almost 30years ago had no potency anymore.

As if reading his thoughts, Nne crushed them with her next words.

"They made me swear a blood oath, Nedum. It was sealed with blood taken from your father. It is very strong in this place and is binding forever till I die. Your Uncle Dike pleaded with them to leave me alone, but they said I had a hand in my husband's death and had to swear the oath to prevent danger for the village. Only God in heaven knows what killed your father. I have no hand in it. They killed him. His people killed him".

"So my son, don't let the curse of the oath strike me dead. That is why I said you cannot marry Anjie. She is a foreigner. Even much more than me. They will make her life hell here. You cannot my son. You cannot", Nne pleaded amidst a fresh stream of tears.

The enormity of what her mother just said sunk home gradually. Like water seeping through a strainer.

It could not be true. It just couldn't be true. All that was ancient history. This was the 60s. People don't just go around forcing people to swear deadly oaths and holding their lives in their hands. No..no way. Whatever it was that happened 27years ago could not now deny him happiness.

Chinedum stood up; munching his lips vigorously. Nne was now silently weeping on the bed, too distraught to even look his son in the face. Too brokenhearted to contemplate the twisted fate that had now pitted her against her son's will.

Her body convulsed with renewed floods of tears; torturing her mind and ripping through her sad soul as her son, who now struggled with fresh demons of his own in a whirlpool mind, walked unsteadily and slowly out of the room.

In the distance, yet more booming, echoing vibrations could be heard as a reminder that a war was going on somewhere beyond the horizon.

CHAPTER SIXTEEN

Riddle: What do you call a sick bird abroad?
Answer: An ill-eagle.

"I know how difficult it is to be new in a strange country. Especially one where you don't speak the language", the host remarked.

He was entertaining the visiting lecturer in his house on his first weekend in South Africa and the vagaries of life in a foreign country was their opening line of discussion.

"Very, very true my dear brother", his guest replied. "Can you imagine how difficult it was to get directions from people? I stopped at the traffic lights near the KFC outlet to get directions to your place and the man in the eatery kept on telling me to turn left at the robot and then I'll get to another robot and there I will make a right turn."

His host was now smiling broadly, obviously enjoying his guest's litany.

"I kept on telling him that there was no robot in the direction where he was pointing, but he didn't listen. How could a robot stand in the middle of the road? Doing what there, I don't know!"

His host was now about to burst out in a muted laughter.

"So", the guest pressed on, "I told him to show me the robot on the road and the next thing he said, 'Are you *kwerekwere*?'. I was just looking like a zombie. I had never heard that word in my life. He just kept on asking, '*kwerekwere?, kwerekwere?*. It was a man who was working behind the counter that now came and asked me where I was from. I told him Nigeria and they both now nodded their heads in agreement. I was about to ask them what Nigeria had to do with my asking for directions when the man from the counter now explained slowly that a robot was the name used here for traffic lights, which was what the first man had been pointing to all along. My brother, I just felt like an idiot!"

His host finally unleashed the laughter swelling up inside him. The guest also joined in, sharing in the comedy of his experience.

"You know what...you know what", the guest continued in between bouts of laughter, "I told myself that how similar our languages are. Do you know that *kwere* in my language means to agree? Incredible, ay?

"Yes", his host agreed, "it is truly an eye-opener for you. I wish you had accepted my offer to pick you up. At least you wouldn't have been forced to listen to such derogatory words".

"Is it derogatory? I thought they said *amakwerekwere* was the name they call Nigerians"

"No ways my friend, *kwerekwere* is used for all foreigners, not only Nigerians".

'Ok, well, it was good I came on my own. At least I have learnt some bit of street language and actually the earlier I start doing that, the better since I will be here for sometime."

"Um, that is right", the host concurred

"And now also I know that a robot in South Africa isn't a machine built like a human being as the rest of the world thinks", the guest announced gleefully.

They downed most of the food and drinks arranged before them on the low table, all the time talking between mouthfuls.

The host lived up to his role quite well and kept on asking his guest if he was okay. If he wanted anything else? If the food was the way he liked it?

Their conversation ranged from the differences between academia in Nigeria and South Africa; to the ease or otherwise of life as a lecturer. Also, they talked about South Africa and its infamous crime rate; the changes in the country since the end of apartheid rule; the impact of the ANC, the ruling party on peoples' lives; the hopes and aspirations of the common citizenry in the government of the day; the standard of living both in the country and in Nigeria; as well as their work in the school in the months ahead.

Just as the guest was thinking of calling it a day and driving back to his own residence, the host said, "I hope you enjoyed our week celebrations last semester".

"Oh that was very well organized. I had a really good time. I however think it was strange that you people choose to announce the new head of department at such a social and informal event. It is not done like that at all in my country".

"Oh", his host responded, "it is also not the tradition here, but I believe Professor Nomvete just wanted to add his own surprise touch to the event. Moreover since the Dean and the school senate had approved it, they normally allow the outgoing person to break the news whichever way he chooses".

"Okay", the guest nodded his understanding. "Why wasn't her husband there with her?"

"Who?"

"I mean the new HOD".

"Oh", the host responded, "I thought you knew. She is not married".

"Oh, ok you mean she is a divorcee"

"Oh no. I've been teaching here for the past nine years and I know she has never been married since she got here about five years ago".

"Oh really! She looks young, though attractive"

"Yes, she is a beautiful woman. No one knows why she never married. Sometimes also men naturally avoid a woman who is 'too educated' in their opinion".

"Yes, I agree, but she is still a Phd holder so I don't think she should intimidate any man who happens to be a lecturer also".

"Well, you might be right but we have always seen her as exceptionally bright. She is very gifted and carries herself well. She will be a handful for any man in the house, though at work she is polite and respectful to everyone of us. Do you know she completed her Phd at 30years of age?"

"Umm, that's impressive".

"Since then, she has written over 15 publications. I have only struggled to publish six. Even Professor Nomvete has only produced 5, so you see how highly we regard her. Actually she is an Associate Professor, but since she hasn't been confirmed, we still call her a doctor".

"That's really impressive", the guest repeated again.

"I believe now that she is the HOD, she will be confirmed. Prof Nomvete always had an eye on her as his successor. In other departments, that could easily have bred bad blood, but here, we all love her. Even though a few of us are much older than her in the department. She is very likeable and gets on well with everyone".

"That is a good thing to hear", added the guest.

"Actually come to think of it, isn't she supposed to have some Nigerian blood in her?"

"Nigerian blood? How come?", the guest sat up at this unexpected piece of intelligence.

"Yes, she is supposed to be half Nigerian or something. I'm not sure, but they say one of her parents was Nigerian and she even spent some time there before we had freedom".

The guest sat transfixed, digesting this news with unusual concentration.

Spent some time in Nigeria?

Since the night of the announcement, he had never been able to overcome the feeling that the new HOD looked quite familiar to him. The problem was where and when?

In his over 28 years academic career, he had taught over two thousand students in six secondary schools, two polytechnics and five universities. All across eight countries in Africa, North America and Europe.

This wealth of experience even compounded his memory the more.

He couldn't of course remember all the thousands of faces of students he had taught but if the new HOD was as bright as he had just been told, then he surely ought not to have forgotten her so easily. She still looked quite young to him, so chances were that she could have sat in front of him in a classroom somewhere, sometime.

"How old is she now?", he asked his host at last. Making it sound like an innocent question.

"Oh Dr Fanteni is about 44-45 now. Not very sure which is the exact age".

44-45? If true, then she must be too old to have been a student of his.

Or was she? He had surely taught a lot of students who were almost as old as himself, so her age didn't automatically disqualify her. But he ought to have remembered her. At least if she was that advanced in years.

The more he juggled his memory, the more blanks he drew.

"Very interesting", the guest remarked again. "Do you know her alma mater?"

"Oh", the host shifted on his cushion, "she attended University of Namibia for her Phd, but I believe she was at Fort Hare for her first and second degrees".

"That is here in South Africa, ay?", the guest wanted to be sure.

"Yes, it is in the Eastern Cape and it is a well-respected institution all over the world".

Well, that ruled her out as a student of his. He surely had not taught in those schools, so the possibility of her being an ex-pupil was a no-brainer.

There were no further leads on the issue of Dr Angelou Fanteni's history and at last, it was time to depart.

The host called out to his wife to come bid their visitor goodbye and after the departure formalities and greetings, the guest got into his car and drove off into the gathering dusk.

CHAPTER SEVENTEEN

Don't ever start what you can't finish

The host had put most of the discussions with their visitor out of his mind and retired to bed beside his plump wife.

Both of them exhausted from the day's numerous exertions.

He was snoring rather noisily but peacefully, when a message beeped its way onto his mobile phone, lying by the lamp hold beside the bed.

He snored on relentlessly. Too far gone in his sleep to be disturbed by the ten second beep-beep from his phone.

If he had woken up to examine the syndicated text message on his phone that night, he would have read the following: **Tx for the reception Sir. Can u kp a secret? I want to tell u that I like ur HOD and I will win her heart. Gnite.**

CHAPTER EIGHTEEN

The highway of life leads in all directions

Anyone familiar with the geography of the land that is today known as Imo State in eastern part of Nigeria, would easily agree that Orogwe is a shouting distance from Owerri, the largest city in the state. The multi-lane highway carrying traffic from burstling, metropolitan Onitsha – 120kms away – connects Orogwe with Owerri. These days, thanks to faster means of automated transport, it takes about 10minutes to reach Owerri from Orogwe.

In 1968 however, there were no multi-lane highways. Neither were there comfortable and quicker vehicles. What there was were mammy-wagons in the 'No Condition Is Permanent' mould – large, clumsy, wooden contraptions that huffed and puffed their way between destinations and ferried all manner of people and goods. They made use of narrow roads which were half-dusty and half-covered with broken asphalt. These roads were built by white, British colonialists who administered Nigeria for almost 100years before granting a grudging independence in October, 1960. They were so narrow in many sections that many a times, mammy-wagons had to stop by the side of the road to allow oncoming traffic to pass. Thus a distance of not more than

10kms, easily ended up taking the better part of two hours. Travel in those days was stop-start, laborious and nothing to look forward to.

It was that sort of inconvenience that Chinedum aimed to avoid that morning, which made him mount a metal bicycle and pedal furiously away from Orogwe; heading to Owerri in search of his beloved Anjie.

He didn't care to take precautions as he rode like a maniac; whizzing past men and machine on the narrow road that snaked through the village of Irete onto Owerri. Sweating and almost blind with fury, his mind was a turmoil of fierce anger as he put distance between himself and the village that now represented a threat to his passionate romance with Anjie.

"Are you ok?", a worried Anjie met him at the entrance of the house. The look on his shiny face told its own story because she had hardly ever seen him in this state and worriedly repeated her question.

"Nedum, what is the matter?", she beseeched him, as he continued to breathe rapidly following his exertions on the road from his village. He was sure he had broken some speed records in getting here but for the moment, he didn't care one bit.

He managed to gush out the revelations Nne made to him that morning, trying his best not to hold anything back. His pain pushed him to pour out the sad tale of his father's demise almost three decades back. His tormented spirit yearned for a comforter on such a difficult day. He longed for a companion; a co-traveller on a journey of self-discovery. On the day his past unraveled starkly before his eyes, he knew only a kindred spirit like Anjie could soothe his wounded soul.

Questions flooded his head that required answers. Urgent answers. From where, he did not know. The only thing he knew at the moment was that he wanted to be with this girl. This girl who had given him love. Who had accepted him for who he was. Who understood him. Who saw him as a life partner; who shared most things with him; who meant to him all things bright and beautiful. Nothing meant anything to him again.

He was convinced about that.

He now knew why he never really belonged at Orogwe. Why he always felt like a stranger looking in. Why conversations ceased and voice levels dropped anytime he approached. Why Nne always insisted he attended school elsewhere – away from the village unlike his peers. Why......

"Oh Nedum...it is alright...it is alright", Anjie's angelic voice interrupted his wild meditation.

"We will find a way to convince Nne, ok?", she assured as if tackling just another minor household problem.

He looked into her eyes and despite himself, he felt strength seeping back into him. How could this innocent-looking girl be so sure where he was clueless?

"And please stop biting your lips. I have told you several times that you will ruin them", she rebuked him softly.

It was a bad habit of his. Lip-biting. He often did it absent-mindedly but it became even more pronounced when he was pondering over a problem. Such as now.

"I'm sorry", he responded. 'I just don't know what we'll do. I thought Nne liked you and was sure she would be happy to see us together. I mean together as husband and wife. I just don't understand all this talk about her swearing an oath. I don't accept it Anjie. It will not work, They cannot separate us. I cannot live without you Anjie", he held her hands, looking deep into her eyes.

"I am sure she does want us together but she is also afraid of the oath", Anjie said.

They debated various ways out of the situation. Anjie suggested they go see Uncle Dike and ask him to intervene and plead with Nne. Chinedum said it was meaningless. That Nne wasn't the problem. It was the threat of what would happen to her if she allowed the oath to be breached. He knew his mother. She wanted him to be happy, but if his happiness now meant she would face dire consequences, she could be forced to deny him.

They eventually shared their dilemma with Aunty Ada.

She shook her head sadly and was quiet for a long time after hearing Chinedum's dilemma.

She had heard of such things. It was common in most rural communities, where the people subjected women and wives married into their households, to vows of all manner. Anybody who took such vows were bound to respect them because breaking them often carried stern consequences. They ranged from severe illness, to epilepsy, madness, blindness and even mysterious deaths.

She felt very sad for Anjie. How unlucky was she that the one man that had stolen her heart could be connected to a fate that made their love forbidden? How very unlucky!

Nonetheless, as the day dragged on and dusk approached, she entreated Chinedum to return home. But not before asking him to inform his mother that she, Ada would pay her a visit. It was time she met his people and see things for herself. Who knows, she and Nne could arrive at a solution which seemed impossible especially as they hardly knew each other. After all, the wise elders say, two heads are always better than one.

With such assurance, she sent Chinedum back to his mother with news of Aunty Ada's impending visit.

CHAPTER NINETEEN

If only we could be like the elephant, nothing would ever be forgotten

"Hello Madam!"

"Hello Mr...sorry Dr Kalu isn't it?", Angelou corrected herself.

"That is right Madam"

"Oh please pardon me. I remember you from the end of year celebrations night last semester".

"That is correct again Madam", he beamed expansively.

"That was three months ago. I didn't expect you would still be around", Angelou gushed.

"Oh actually, my presence that night coincided with the start of my sabbatical here. I will be here at UJ for the whole academic session", Dr Kalu revealed.

Something about this polished woman kept needling his memory.

"Oh that's very good. So we should be seeing much more of you then", she remarked.

"Yes Madam. I'm actually with the History department. That is my speciality in Nigeria".

"Oh ok, that's great. I remember you are the deputy dean of the School of Arts at Port Harcourt in Nigeria?", she recollected perfectly.

"Yes, you have a good memory Madam. Except that we call it faculty over there"

"Oh, ok not much different from ours though, except in name I believe".

"Yes Madam. If I may ask, have you ever been in Nigeria?"

The question took Angelou completely by surprise but she had been expecting it since that night this man walked into the hall three months back.

She had hoped his visit would be brief and there would have been no opportunity for the two of them to swap any stories about Nigeria.

"Oh yes", she responded smoothly. "I actually spent my early life there".

"Really, that's quite interesting. Mr Tshabalala mentioned it in passing last week when he hosted me at his place that you had some Nigerian blood in you".

"Oh, well it is an open secret here", she replied coyly.

"So how often do you go back to visit?", he pressed on, pleased with the fruits of his enquiry.

"Oh not often. I'm always too busy here and the work I do as well as several other commitments take too much of my time. So where do you stay? Here in UJ?", she changed the subject deftly.

"Oh, I stay in town. They gave me a small apartment at a place in town called Joe Slovo Avenue. It is close to the Ellis Park stadium. It belongs to the school"

"Oh ok, I know the place. Yes it belongs to the school and lots of other students rent apartments there also".

"So how are you finding your new appointment?", he persisted, refusing to be put off track.

"Oh that. It isn't quite new to me anymore. I've been into it now for over three months".

They were standing in the staff parking lot opposite the huge library block, where she sometimes left her car whenever she wanted to use the private reading rooms.

Already, she couldn't wait to exit from his presence and his prying eyes.

"If you don't mind doctor, I have a History of Medieval Literature class in a couple of minutes and I don't like to keep them waiting", she spoke up.

"That is okay. It is unusual though that you still handle lectures despite being a HOD".

"I am first a lecturer and secondly, whatever office I find myself occupying. My primary calling is to teach", she smiled sweetly.

"That is good to know. Most people in your position would be very reluctant to handle the chalk and stand in front of a class anymore", he retorted, impressed by her principles.

"Well, I am Angelou Fanteni, not 'most people', so I have to do what I believe is right with my conscience. Moreover, the department is a bit short of hands at the moment so I have to chip in with my time to help the remaining teachers", she clarified.

"That is really kind of you".

"Im only doing what I'm paid to do. Have a good day Dr Kalu and see you around".

"Yes, Madam, I really look forward to us meeting again. Probably we could arrange something during the weekend so we can sit down to talk, ay?", he ventured hopefully.

"Ok, we'll see", she replied hurriedly, as she slid behind the wheel and navigated out of the park leaving him standing in a thin cloud of rising, red dust.

Breathing steadily, she knew she couldn't allow this stranger to get too close.

She would kill Tshabalala when she saw her next. What cheek going round discussing her life with a complete stranger. Well, the man always looked deadbeat and she wouldn't have ascribed that much intelligence to him. He was surely the last person on earth she could think would know anything about her.

How very much she had underrated him, she mused.

Her phone shrieked to life in her bag, forcing her to apply the brakes automatically but slowly, as she picked up the bag with one hand, searching inside for the Nokia 3310.

It wasn't a call.

It was a reminder that she had to go to the Home Affairs department on Market Street in an hour's time to submit an application for a civil marriage.

Between her and Rupert Mabizela.

She smiled.

That was surely a timely reminder.

Something to take her mind away from the pock nosing antics of Tshabalala and his Nigerian accomplice.

CHAPTER TWENTY

When in love, always trust your heart

"Whao Angel, you are a curious one indeed", Big V remarked cheerily in between huge gulps of hot cappucino.

Angelou was having a steamy mug of Rooibos tea, which was a staple of hers whenever they met like this. The three musketeers, as they liked to joke amongst themselves.

"Well, a girl has to follow her heart sometime in her life", Angelou replied her.

"A girl? You should be saying a granny!", Big V teased

"No, a girl, with a big G", Maria came to her friend's support.

"Okay, I agree with you two. So have they given you a date now?" Big V plunged in.

"Sure. It is the 15th of June. I hope you guys will be free that day. I need you both there", Angelou piped up, her eyes gleaming in anticipation.

They were all in Gordarts, giggling and laughing like teenagers.

Since that unforgettable night with Rupert on the sofa in her lounge room, Angelou had known she couldn't carry on without Rupert firmly in her life. Solidly by her side.

She worshipped him like her own skin, she had gushed to Maria and Big V the following day as she narrated a watered-down version of her intimate escapade with Rupert.

They both stared at her aghast. Hardly believing most of what she told them.

Though she tried her utmost best to keep out the steamy details from her narration, the two other women knew exactly what might have happened on that sofa, that night.

They were no spring chickens. They understood the rapid changes their friend's life was going through and were mature enough to see that her heart was fully in it.

Maria had even done some surreptitious investigations of her own about Rupert and it yielded nothing heartbreaking. He truly had no girlfriends any where in the school and as best as Angelou herself could find out from asking him, he had none anywhere else.

He was equally devoted to her. Notwithstanding the fifteen years difference between them, he played the role of a doting lover and partner perfectly.

He had been shocked of course when Angelou had first broached the issue of marriage. He actually had looked afraid at the thought of it. But as she gave him time to think about it and to consider the fact that she may not be able to give him a child due to her age, he gradually came to terms with the idea.

She never put any pressure on him. Always allowing him to express his feelings to her anytime and any how he felt. His maturity and ease of manner made the transition from student into lover, seamless.

She gave him more freedom and access to her house. Often coming back from work to find him immersed in the process of cooking up a delicacy in his kitchen.

Maria and Big V also gradually came to accept him and respect his new role in their friend's life. Despite her elevation to HOD, Angelou had not changed towards them one bit. She still craved their presence and company and considered their counsels with great regard.

They were proud of her. Proud of her progress. Happy for what she stood for and where she had got to in her career.

Happier more were they about the entrance of Rupert into her life. Angelou's rise and rise represented a pleasant beacon to them. A reminder that no mountain was too high enough to stop one reaching their dreams and desires.

To them both, Angelou had overcome great odds to get to where she was today. She had conquered. She had overcome. She was a heroine who was not only self-made, but equally humble and self-effacing in her hour of glory.

Her accomplishments were to them, as glittering as they was laudable. Though she always dismissed it, they knew her present status also conferred on her considerable wealth and prosperity. Just two months back, she confided in them both that she was negotiating the purchase of a 30acre farm in a small village outside Empangeni in the Kwazulu Natal province. An investment such as that had all the trappings of an egg-nest.

That Angelou had found love; true love at such a late stage of her life reassured them that the impossible could very much become possible. That no force in the world could stop an episode whose time had come. To them, if

Angelou's life was a revelation, the coming of Rupert into it was a revolution of unparalleled proportions.

Accordingly, they gave her their unalloyed support. They cocooned her relationship with Rupert with all jealous zeal. Determined to see it come to fruition and metamorphose into a testimony of unheralded fidelity. A shining example of love knowing no boundaries.

It was therefore with girlish anticipation that they all looked forward to the day, June 15th 2000, when their friend, Angelou Fanteni would be joined together in an extraordinary but loving matrimony.

Rupert's father couldn't make the long trip from Kimberley to Johannesburg for the ceremony but there was an uncle who lived at Germiston on the outskirts of the city and he had been contacted. After some awkwardness due to Angelou's age, he had agreed to be there on confirmation with Mabizela Senior that the union had his blessing.

Angelou in consultation with the two other 'musketeers', also decided to inform Professor Nomvete out of respect to him.

They had all gone along in Maria's car that evening to see the old man at his humble house in Illovo – a plush part of the city. After listening to their story, he sighed deeply and invited Angelou separately into his bedroom. He had always liked her and treated her sometimes like his own daughter. But this development mystified him.

He knew the intending groom however and had taught him four years back when he first came in as a fresh student. He knew his academic abilities as well, but as he lectured Angelou in the inner recesses of his room that evening, he advised that her that if she was sure in her heart that the young man wanted nothing else from her expect her love, he was happy to approve their union.

So with all likely obstacles cleared, the three friends tied all loose ends to what would be an epochal day not only in the life of Angelou, but in all their lives as well.

CHAPTER TWENTY ONE

Success is never final, neither is failure fatal. But courage is what counts

It was now just a week before the wedding appointment with the Home Affairs.

Bride and bridegroom were as restless and fidgety as clothes hung on a line.

Angelou especially. She never in her wildest imaginations thought she would live to ever be any man's wife. Not at her age anyway.

Though she secretly longed for a partner. Someone to share her dreams and aspirations; as well, she knew time was very much not on her side.

Since her ill-fated romance almost thirty years back, marital life for her had remained a mirage. Something to be desired but almost, always out of reach.

She had always nursed the hope that she would meet someone who would re-ignite the flames of love in her heart. But as her early days in this new country rolled into months and onto years, nothing in that wise happened.

Not that she was short of suitors. Her dazzling beauty and impressive manners attracted scores of men folk, but Angelou was always wary in matters of the heart.

Having been badly-burnt back in Nigeria, she treaded carefully in the realm of relationships. She saw most men as hunters in search of prey, who were very skilled at hiding their true intentions. Accordingly, she regarded all of them suspiciously.

Throughout her school days at Fort Hare, hardly any two or three months passed by without her fending off the advances of eager-beaver male students. Those of them who were hoping she would be an easy catch, quickly gave up the chase when they realized she was a hard nut to swallow. Let alone crack.

The very few who persevered and bid their time, hardly fared better.

Angelou Fanteni was not about to be anyone's trophy. She resisted and warded off every male overture throughout her six-year stay at Fort Hare; so much so that at the point of graduation a few wicked rumours were being spread that she was gay.

Not that it bothered her though. In her heart of hearts, she knew if the right man came, she would know. And she would yield.

After Fort Hare and onto the small private college in Hermanus in the deprived part of Western Cape where she taught for a couple of years, male attention still trailed her.

It continued all the way to Windhoek, where she spent another 19months studying for a fulltime doctorate degree.

She had fond memories of her time at the University of Namibia, which was like a second home of sorts to her. Considering the transitory, befuddled time she had spent in the country during her harrowing journey almost three decades back, Namibia had a poignant place in her life. And in her mind. But Namibia neither yielded any Mr Right.

For her though, just any relationship would not do.

She was not the type of woman to compromise just for the sake of any male company. Just like the saying back home: better to have a well-nourished frog for food if one would descend so low at to have one at all.

This stubborn principle stuck with her through all the years she spent building both her career and profile. All manner of men sought her hand. All failed.

By the time she arrived at Johannesburg University, the watershed age of 40 had been reached. For her, as with most women her age, romance and courtship now seemed a bridge too far. Unlike most women her age however, she stubbornly believed that her destiny still harboured something more dramatic than the life of a frustrated crone.

What she lacked in a mutual relationship however, she made up for in achievements.

Her career path, which had always been on an upward trajectory, skyrocketed at UJ.

Promotions, appointments, awards and scholarly endowments came in a steady flood. She excelled in all that she was entrusted with and her gifts shone brilliantly.

After just three years at UJ, she was sitting on the Faculty of Arts academic board. This was also coupled with her post as Interim president of the white-dominated South African Alliance of Literary and Debating Societies. Added to these were her promotion to the position of a Reader in her department; National Vice-President of the Nardine Gordimer Book Club; Associate Director of the Institute of African Literary Studies, headquartered in Nairobi, Kenya; recipient of the Leopold Senghor award for African Literature Excellence; and also the post of a judge on the highly-prestigious BBC African Book Prize annual awards panel.

As far as the eye could see, Angelou Fanteni was a shining star of celebrity proportions. And both staff and students of the entire University of Johannesburg celebrated her as an icon.

Their icon.

Though strengthened with a fierce inner belief that she would not spend the rest of her days devoid of a loving male partner, it was still with infinite relief and boundless delight that she welcomed the arrival of Rupert into her life. He represented everything she wanted in a man.

All her secret and often-suppressed expectations of a male companion were embodied in his character. He was appealing, charming, polite, understanding, patient and quite mature. All this on top of the obvious fact that he was academically, a mastermind.

Angelou, in all her quiet supplications to God, couldn't have asked for a better deal in the romance stakes. If he was the answer to her prayers, she was totally fulfilled.

He spoke and acted far and ahead of his age. Despite having lost his mother at an early age, he also had impeccable upbringing as she found out. His story about being an only child put her on the same keel with Angelou and served as a useful foundation for both their interaction.

She had gone with him to visit his uncle, Dumisani at his one-room apartment in Germiston several times and though initially wary of her, the aging ex-railway worker had seen the glint in both their eyes and given them a tacit blessing.

Through no fault of hers, series of efforts to visit Mabizela Snr in faraway Kimberley never materialized. However, she and Rupert had spoken to the old man severally over the phone and she promised that they would come out to see him in the summer, when she would be on her annual vacation.

As it finally became a *fait accompli* to her that her young suitor-cum-student would soon become her better half, Angelou decided on a heirloom for him. Something he would own and keep on both their behalfs and in case they both produced any offsprings - of which she was quite skeptical - something to pass onto them.

Without consulting anyone about it, Angelou instructed her lawyers to draw up a will.

The document was finally ready for her inspection and approval on June 3rd, 2000.

It was with deep satisfaction therefore that she received her copy that morning on her office table – noting with utmost contentment that all her life's struggles and labour, when quantified in monetary terms was now worth a tidy R16,788,009 million.

If she dropped dead now, all that would belong to him. All of it.

She trusted him that much.

CHAPTER TWENTY TWO

I am what I am and what I am is me.

"I think it will be best if you have one of your trusted friends there with you"

"Are you very sure about that?"

"Of course I am sure my dear. Why do you ask?"

"I was just wondering if you wanted anyone there. Or anyone to know, especially..."

"Oh come off it", she cut him short. "I'm not doing anything secretly. And I'm certainly not doing anything wrong, so why do I need to hide?".

"No I didn't mean you should hide. I just thought you might not want anyone, especially students to know yet", he argued tamely.

"I'm not in denial my dear. At least not about you. I'm proud of what I'm doing. I'm happy to be your wife. I'm happy. I'm excited. I'm over the moon. It means everything to me and I don't care what anyone thinks, nothing is going to spoil my special day".

They were sitting in her car. A grey, sturdy Isuzu bakkie. It was quite unfashionable for women to be seen driving bakkies but Angelou always bucked the trend. It gave her a thrill. An adrenalin rush to swim against the grain. She had always been her own person. So taking on dos and donts was second nature to her.

Actually the fact that a thing was frowned upon, made it attractive to her.

Just like women riding bakkies.

Marrying Rupert also was very much in line with that sort of attitude.

Which was part of what dominated their discussion as they sat and watched the winter sun descend over the edge of the Melville Koppies. Just behind the small, but well-maintained Eben Cuyler park.

"So don't get worked up over who knows and who doesn't. I will be with you for the rest of our lives anyway, so the earlier the whole world knows, the better for everyone. Ok?"

"Ok, Maam", he responded with relief.

"And please, please I'm not Maam. Not to you at least".

"Well, it sounds awkward I agree but I think I need time to adjust to my new status".

That was one of the things she liked about him. Modest and polite to a fault.

She turned round in her seat to fully look at him.

"I love you very much Rupert. I truly do from the bottom of my heart and I don't want to ever, ever be without you"

Even at his age, he still felt a bit embarrassed at this kind of special attention.

Turning also, he gathered her in his huge arms and cuddled her as best as the space afforded them by the steering wheel in front of her.

They stayed in that position for what seemed an eternity.

Then she asked if him who he would like to accompany him to the ceremony at Home Affairs.

"I hope you approve of him, but I'm thinking of asking Napoleon".

She almost burst out laughing.

"You mean you cannot think of anyone else in the entire school?"

"Well, you know I don't have too many friends, but among the few I have, he is my best friend".

"Are you serious?"

"I am Maam", he replied before realizing his mistake and winking an apology at her.

After reflecting for a few seconds, she said: "I never knew you two were that friendly".

"Oh I'm sure I've mentioned him in the past. He is much more trustworthy than most of the other people you see in the class. His jokes often give people a very wrong impression of him".

"Really?"

"Really. He is a good man and I promise you, he'll be the least surprised person in the world to know Mrs HOD is hooking up one of her students. He has a 19year-old fiancée that he is absolutely crazy about".

"Umm, very interesting. I never knew you two were such chums. You will have to invite him for the small reception at Gordart after the Home Affairs thing then. Like I told you, we will be hosting a few friends there to celebrate with us. Professor Nomvete, Maria, Vivian and a few of the lecturers from the department will be there as well. I guess Napoleon will be the only student there. But jokes are not on the menu for sure", she stressed, smiling at him.

"We all still wonder how you shut him up though the other day with that riddle of yours. Napoleon knows all the riddles and jokes in the world", he looked at her in askance.

"Well my dear, he must have had you all coiled round his finger. Some of us know a few also. Like, in which country is everyone always hungry?"

"That must be Somalia", he replied confidently.

"Wrong. It is Hungary!"

"Whao! You really are into it, ay?", he looked at her, impressed.

"Ok, what about this? Why did Moses in the Bible lose the race to the Promised Land?"

"No idea. I give up", he conceeded.

"Fine. Because the Lord asked him to come forth!"

"Whao, whao, whao!", he looked even more impressed.

"One last one for you. What part of the army is full of babies? Well I can see you have no clue. The answer is Infantry!".

He just shook his head in disbelief, grimacing broadly at her all the time.

They still remained cuddled and after another quiet interlude, Rupert squeezed loose and asked her: "Did you ever regret leaving Nigeria? I mean after all these years?"

She wasted no time before replying.

"Not one bit. Of course I miss my aunt and her children because they were all the family I had but I'm glad I left, though I had very little choice in the matter. I have no idea what my life would have been like if I had stayed, but I'm thankful where I am today. Especially where I am sitting beside the most wonderful man in the world!".

He smiled appreciatively.

Though she had told him her story several times, he still felt a tinge of pity for her having to leave home at such a young age into an unknown future.

But she had proved herself a strong and independent woman and he never missed the chance to assure her that age difference notwithstanding, he would stand by her for the rest of their lives.

June 15 couldn't come soon enough for them both.

CHAPTER TWENTY THREE

The moment of final truth is always a moment of final freedom

At exactly 7.45pm on the night of June 10, Dr Kalu finally solved the riddled that had become an obsession to him since the night of the Dramatics Arts department week celebrations, eight months ago.

The obsession had developed a life of its own the more he saw the new HOD of the Dramatic Arts department. She truly was a stunning woman. The type all men; red blooded men that is, would want to covet as their own.

Though his mission in South Africa was purely academical and he had little or no contact with her since they were in different departments, his interest in her steadily grew to become a love interest.

He liked the woman. Having been divorced for the past five years himself, he had given little thought and attention to intimate female liaison. With his two boys now grown up and living separately but independently in different parts of Nigeria, he felt no binding need to nurture a relationship with another woman. Until now.

He wasn't a womanizer. But this woman touched all the raw nerves in him. She clicked all the right points.

More intriguing to him was the knowledge that she hailed partly from Nigeria. It pricked his interest deeply and on closer inspection, her face stirred something he had known long, long ago. Something he felt very strongly he had been part of.

After he accosted her that afternoon at the parking lot, and squeezed a confirmation from her that truly, she had once lived in Nigeria, his curiosity had gone into overdrive.

Coupled with his romantic interest in her, he had plunged into the unassigned task of unearthing Angelou Fanteni's past.

He sought out Tshabalala again by paying him visits at his place. But his slow-thinking friend couldn't divulge more than he had already told him during that initial visit.

Tshabalala was still amused about the contents of the sms Dr Kalu had sent him that night and the two men often laughed over it. For Kalu however, it was no laughing matter.

He really liked the woman.

His desire to win her pushed him to attempt many devices to gain her attention and interest. He called her office several times in the day asking to speak with her. The few times when her secretary admitted she was on seat and put her on to speak with him, she managed to rebuff all his offers of a date.

Exasperated after series of attempts over three months, he had asked around for her residence. No one seemed to know. Or better still, because he had a foreign accent, people were wary of him asking about a senior colleague's address and therefore pretended not to know.

He even tried attending one of the lectures he was sure she was handling, but the classes were always too full and all the seats taken. The thought of standing through an entire hour in a humid classroom full of chattering students proved too much for him to contemplate.

Once when he cornered her on her way out of a class, she fended him off with the excuse that she had to chair a pre-examination meeting and was already late.

To the best of his limited abilities and without making himself look stupid, he tried everything humanly possible to get the HOD's attentions.

All failed.

Exasperated, he had decided on another course of action.

The more time he spent pursuing Angelou and the more he saw of her, the more convinced he was that he had seen her somewhere, sometime in the past.

He thought deep and hard about this mystery and replayed with all care every country, every school and every place he had taught in the past 28years.

Nothing seemed to click as days turned into weeks and further lengthened into months. When it looked as if his recollections would lead him nowhere, he stumbled on something remote and forgotten, which greatly stirred his overworked brain.

One cold evening, sitting at his reading table and looking through an outdated group picture back from his school days in 1963, his eyes rested on the face of his late, childhood friend Chinedum.

The black-and-white, now-turning-brown snapshot was taken behind a derelict school building in Owerri, eastern Nigeria, before the Nigerian civil war.

Chinedum Okoroafor. How could he ever forget him?

He had a small group of friends back then. Especially as a keen sportsman and leader of the Native Band Group in the school, he wasn't lacking in acquaintances. Many attimes, he was chosen by several teachers – Masters they were called in those days – to discipline errant junior students due to his position of authority.

It was just about the time they were preparing for Cambridge final exams that he took the picture with some of his classmates, of which Chinedum was one of them.

His friend's trademark smile in the fading picture was in stark contrast to the ill fortune that befell him years later after they had left school and were all either working or engaged in trading.

Suddenly, he paused. Yes! Yes! That was it. That was what kept on drifting in and out of his memory since he arrived South Africa over eight months back.

How on earth could he have missed it? How on earth?

Despite it being right there before his eyes all this time.

How could he have failed to make the connection?

God! He must be getting old.

He sat still for a long, long time as if struck by paralysis.

Shaking his head over and over again, he couldn't believe the incredible coincidence he was now finally coming to terms with.

At last, he grabbed his hold-all; yanked it open and commenced a frantic, excited search for something. Hoping against all odds that he would find it

After rummaging through the ancient bag, he found it to his colossal relief.

It was a small, white complimentary card. The type which carried names, telephone numbers, addresses and sometimes a headshot picture.

This one bore no picture. But the number on it was precious enough.

It was a Nigerian office number that he was sure would shed more light on this unbelievable mystery he was about to solve.

He reached for the digital phone receiver on his reading table.

Then he took a deep, deep breathe.

He punched in the number on the card and then placed the receiver on his ear.

4400kms away in Port-Harcourt, Nigeria, an international call came through, announcing itself with the shrill ringing of a table telephone in a quiet, church office.

CHAPTER TWENTY FOUR

'He is risen. He is risen and He lives forever more'

"Hello? Hello? Yes? Oh doctor, it's you", a grating, hoarse voice answered.

"Yes it's me", Dr Kalu's voice responded from 4400kms away.

"Ah, how is South Africa? Since you left last year, you have not even bothered to call us. Have you forgotten us already?", the voice croaked on.

"How can I? I'm sorry Reverend. I'm really sorry. Things have been very hectic here since I came", Dr Kalu explained.

"Doctor, doctor. It is really a surprise hearing from you. Even though we couldn't see before you left, my archdeacon told me that he attended the small send-off they held for you at the Presidential Hotel. He said you sent your greetings to me through him", the croaky voice drawled.

"Yes Reverend. I told him to greet you. How is he now?", Dr Kalu enquired.

"Oh we thank God for his life but we believe he is right now resting in the bosom of our Lord Jesus Christ", the man with the croaky voice made a sign of the cross, while uttering the last part of his mini-speech.

"What? You mean he is dead?", Dr Kalu blurted out.

"Yes doctor, he passed away three months ago. I believe it was in March. Pardon me.....let me get my glasses and check the date for you. I marked it here on the wall calendar", Croaky voice pleaded.

"Oh please accept my condolences Sir. Can you give my regards to the Archbishop and the rest of the church? I will call again soon to speak personally with him. Oh God!", Dr Kalu wailed audibly into the phone.

Croaky voice sat numbly with his varicosed right hand gripping the receiver. Oblivious of his caller's own state of anxiety, he proceeded to relate how sick the Archdeacon had been for the past six months; how the church had got him admitted at the University of Nigeria Teaching Hospital, Enugu at considerable cost; how he had been transferred from Umuahia to Port Harcourt to relieve the sick archdeacon; how he missed Umuahia after having spent the past 11years there; how he hoped the church would quickly find a replacement for the departed archdeacon here in Port Harcourt in order for him to return to his beloved Umuahia.

Due to the Reverend's advanced age, he spoke slowly. Picking his words one after the other. Though slightly irritated, Dr Kalu maintained his cool to hear him out.

At last, the Reverend came to the end of his monologue and asked:

"So doctor, how is life with you over there?"

"Oh Reverend, I'm grateful for everything. I actually called to ask you a few questions Sir".

"Yes? I'm available to help".

"Sir, do you remember Chinedum Okoroafor?"

"Is he a preacher here?" the ancient, croaky voice asked in return.

"No, no Reverend, he used to be one of your members at Orogwe before the war, remember?".

"Oh my son, it is a longtime now. Was he a soldier?"

"Oh Father, he was not a soldier. He was my friend. Remember his mother, Nne Okoroafor, who lost her husband and was forbidden to remarry. Remember also that Chinedum was supposed to marry one Yoruba girl, who later died just few days to their wedding. You presided at the burial. I was there father. You..."

"It is true my son", he cut him short. "Yes...yes I remember him. What sad story. In all my fifty-two years as a servant of the Lord I never witnessed anything as miserable as the story of that young man. But he is dead also now, isn't it?"

"Yes Father, he died long, long ago. I think it is about twenty years now. We were good friends Reverend. But the reason I called you sir is to tell you that I think I've found his wife", Dr Kalu announced with caution. Almost whispering the news over the phone.

"His wife? Was he married?", the Reverend asked ignorantly.

"No, I mean the Yoruba girl. The one he was supposed to marry that died in 1968. The one you conducted her burial".

"You mean you have seen the dead body? In South Africa?"

"No father. Not the dead body. She is alive. Here in South Africa", Dr Kalu couldn't contain himself any longer. "She is alive Father. I think it's her. I'm sure it's her!".

"Doctor, doctor", the old man responded speculatively, gripping the receiver even more tightly. "Doctor Kalu, are you sure you are okay?".

116

"I am okay Reverend. I have seen her with my two eyes. She is alive here! She is in the same school where I teach! Oh father, it is a miracle!", he continued breathlessly.

"Doctor, what has come over you? If I didn't know you very well, I would say you were high on something. But God forbid that I pass judgement on a good man like you. Dr Kalu are you saying that girl is alive? That girl I buried myself over thirty years ago? I remember the drama that happened that day. How Chinedum jumped into the grave and said he wanted to die with the girl. I never saw anything like it. It was as if he was possessed that evening. How can you now say the girl is alive? Please doctor, if this is a joke, I don't think it is funny. I only know of one person who died and rose up again. And that person was a man, not a woman and his name is Jesus Christ, the son of God", the Reverend insisted vehemently; rounding up his speech.

Dr Kalu was getting slightly annoyed now.

"Father, remember I was also there on that day. It was during the war but things were still not bad at Orogwe and Owerri then. At least we could still go to work and farm. I was there also Father, that day and was one of the people who took Nedum home after he fainted. But Father, I've seen the girl. I was confused myself for a long time after I saw her here. She now has a South African name and speaks their language perfectly. But Father, I spoke to her myself and she confessed...."

"Confessed that she rose from the dead?", the Reverend interrupted.

"No Father. She confessed that she is from Nigeria but left a long, long time ago".

Both men carried on their divergent dialogue like this for almost half an hour and though still unconvinced,

Reverend Desmond Madu agreed to assist Dr Kalu by searching for the one person who would help explain this incredible mystery.

He knew she still lived in Owerri after all these years.

Before hanging up, Dr Kalu extracted a promise from the tired but now-curious cleric to send someone to go to Owerri and invite a former member of his parish, Aunty Adanna, to come see him at Port Harcourt. If anyone could shed light on this great mystery, she would be the one.

The wizened cleric, still shaken and dazed by all he had heard over the phone in the past hour, asked Dr Kalu to him call back in two days; by which time he would have some news for him.

CHAPTER TWENTY FIVE

The calm always preceeds the storm

Everything was now set for the small ceremony billed for the Home Affairs.

Maria and Big V had taken it upon themselves to make sure nothing failed. They had redecorated the small café at Gordarts with bright buntings and balloons ahead of the mini-reception that would hold there straight from the Home Affairs.

Angelou insisted it remained small because she wanted to attract little or no attention to herself.

Her friends protested long and hard, but she stood her ground and made it clear that she didn't want a crowd. After debating to and fro for days, they all finally settled on a guest list of just eight – including the celebrants of course.

Though it was her big day and she looked forward to revelling in it, she still didn't want it turned into a market scene. Known for being a private person, Angelou shunned excessive noise and too many people in the same room at the same time always made her uneasy.

Even her wedding day would have to succumb to that rule.

But she was really thrilled and couldn't stop smiling and laughing as the great day approached. Maria and Vivian never stopped teasing her. Needling her about what colour and type of dress she would wear and all the other frilly-dilly stuff that women get so worked up about.

They almost had a fit when she teased them back by saying she was considering going to the occasion in her Converse jeans and a well-ironed check shirt.

"I'll be the first person to strip you naked right there before everyone Angel. You wouldn't dare turn up on your wedding day in such outfit". Maria warned.

"You want to bet?", Angelou dared her with a mischievous smile playing on her lips.

"Of course I do want to bet you wouldn't dare", Maria stood up to her challenge jokingly.

"Ok, let's see who will lose this time. Its not me mind you", Angelou teased her further.

"I will make sure you don't win of course by coming over to your place and throwing all your jeans and shirts into the washing machine. How about that?", Maria threatened.

"I'm sure you wouldn't do something like that just to win a bet".

"And I'm sure you wouldn't do something like going to your wedding in jeans just to prove a point", Maria countered.

They taunted each other like this endlessly and swapped jokes as they sat in Angelou's office. They all, including Big V talked about nothing else these days.

It was the centerpiece of their lives now. The topic of all their discussions. Nothing else mattered to them anymore.

Angelou even told them both how Napoleon reacted when Rupert asked him to be his best man at the ceremony.

"Imagine that naughty boy", Angelou began. "He told Rupert that he would only consider coming if he was allowed to kiss me after the wedding. What cheek!"

"Well, can't blame him. All the boys in the class must wish they were in Rupert's shoes", Big V said.

"Well, they better keep dreaming. I'm still their HOD and no amount of change in marital status will make them get closer to me", Angelou responded cheerily.

"So did he agree to come?", Maria wanted to know.

"Oh he did, but like I told Rupert to tell him, no jokes for the day. He still managed to actually squeeze Rupert's hands though and requested that we also attend his *lobola* thing next semester. He's getting hooked to this sweet 19year-old. You should see her. Rupert showed me her picture. She is lovely. One thing though, I'm sure we will all finally get to know his real name on that day!".

"Whao, looks like everyone in the department is catching the wedding bug", Big V piped up.

"Yea, everyone except we two old rockers", Maria eyed Big V.

While they were chit-chatting, Angelou considered telling them about the overtures she had been subjected to recently by the visiting Nigerian lecturer from History department.

When she had discussed it with Rupert, he had asked her if she knew him back in Nigeria. Of course her answer was negative. The only people she knew in Nigeria, she was sure, would either be all dead now or way too old to have any tangible memories of her. Well, most of them anyway.

As usual, she was self-assured that like all the others before him, the Nigerian lecturer would eventually give up the chase and join the rest of his kind on the dunghill of rejection.

After considering it, she eventually dismissed the idea of telling her friends. No point flogging a dead horse. It was a time of all-round excitement and she didn't want to sour the atmosphere with something that could not in any way affect her long-awaited date with destiny.

One thing she did readily share with them was her honeymoon destination after the wedding. She and Rupert had chosen the Comoros Islands after she showed him a couple of catalogues from her regular travel agency. She had been there on her own a couple of times. Once during a UNESCO regional conference and the second time for a meeting of the SADCC educational council, as part of the Vice-Chancellor's team.

They were both enjoyable experiences and she wanted to share them with the special man in her life. Both of them alone this time.

The only downside of the beautiful island was its *lingua franca*. French was the language of communication and it could be very cumbersome for a non-speaker like her. Nonetheless, the staff of L'Hotel La Tropicana at Moroni always did their utmost to make every guest feel at home and she was sure they would be up to the task this time around. Already, they were expecting her and her new groom.

One day therefore, long after all this, she would tell Maria and Vivian about the lascivious Dr Kalu and they would all have a laugh over it.

CHAPTER TWENTY SIX

The heart of man is desperately wicked; can you know it?

Just as he was about to round up for the day, the long-awaited call came through from Nigeria. He almost missed it because he was already at the door of his office; on his way out. Eager to get home and make himself dinner after another stressful day dealing with examination scripts.

It was just after 6pm but it was already dark and lights had come on in almost all the empty offices adjacent to his. They say it was like that in wintertime here and he could understand why everyone always seemed in a rush to get home from 4-5pm. The cold was not friendly to any outdoor activity at this time of the year.

He was at the door going out when the phone on his table started ringing.

At first he thought of ignoring it. The caller would have to leave a voice message for him to listen tomorrow morning. On a second thought however, he changed his mind and reached for it.

"Hello, hello? Oh Reverend it's you. How are you Sir?".

"I am strong by His grace. How are you too? Listen Doctor, I think you might be right after all. The girl is truly alive as you said".

Waves of excitement coursed through his veins.

"Did you find anything Sir?".

"My dear doctor, I found a lot. The girl is truly alive. It is an incredible story. The type of which I've never heard of in all my 76years", Reverend Madu declared.

"Please Sir, what is the latest? I'm eager to know everything Sir", Dr Kalu pleaded.

"It is true as you said doctor. She is alive. I spoke to her auntie. Her name is Ada and she confessed everything to me. She said her name was Anjola. The girl's name I mean. She said she was used by the devil and the boy's mother".

"Which boy, Sir?", Dr Kalu was finding it very hard to restrain himself now.

"Your friend, Nedum, who should have married the girl. Ada said she was used by the boy's mother, Nne Okoroafor. It was a terrible thing they did to that girl. Ada kept on weeping throughout her confession, begging me for forgiveness. She said she has never known peace since that time. That she lost both her children and she has been in and out of hospitals battling one illness or the other".

"What exactly did she say Reverend?", Dr Kalu was getting exasperated with the old man.

"Listen to me doctor. My secretary was with me throughout the whole confession. He took notes of everything the poor woman said and we have a record at the office. Give me a fax number if you can and I will ask him to send it to you first thing in the morning. What time is it over there now?".

"It is almost 7pm now Reverend", Dr Kalu replied speedily as if the connection was at the risk of being broken any second now.

"Ok, let me have your fax number. You will get the whole story tomorrow".

Hurriedly, Dr Kalu dictated the office fax number to the servant of God, who made him repeat it thrice to be sure he got the numbers correct.

"Dr Kalu, please I want to thank you for this act of mercy that you have embarked upon. If not for you, we would have all been deceived by this wicked woman called Nne Okoroafor and Ada. But you see, the holy book says God is not mocked....whatsoever a man soweth so shall he reap. I will hope to hear from you soon again doctor. You have done us all a great service and may the good Lord reward you bountifully".

Dr Kalu failed to hear the 'Amen' uttered by the Reverend at the end of his short prayer.

He failed to hear because already, the beginnings of a clever plan to finally make Angelou Fanteni, HOD of Dramatic Arts department his own, was forming in his mind.

CHAPTER TWENTY SEVEN

The moment you settle for less, you get even less than you deserve

Naturally, Dr Kalu hardly slept a wink all night.

He twisted and turned endlessly in his huge Bradlows bed and even though it was freezing cold everywhere else, he felt very hot and uncomfortable all night.

What could the Reverend have found out? What manner of terrible thing had happened to bring Anjola – that was her real name truly – back from the dead? Was that why the woman kept avoiding him like that?

He must have checked his bedside clock a million times. Willing time to fly and usher in daylight. He felt like a prisoner trapped by time in the house. He of course drifted off to sleep several times, but they were always very brief, troubled and intermittent.

For all his bother and restlessness ironically, he woke up very late.

By the time he managed to drag himself out of the huge poster bed and take a hot shower, get dressed and drive the short, two kilometers to the university, he had missed his first lecture for the day which started at 9.30am.

Breathlessly, he stormed into his office and true to the Reverend's words, there were two long sheets of fax paper carrying the eagerly-awaited message from Nigeria, hanging loose from the beeping machine.

He yanked it out, locked the door and sat down panting on his revolving chair.

CONFESSION OF MRS ADANNA MATTHEW, PARISHIONER.
MADE THIS DAY, JUNE 11TH, 2000 AT THE CHURCH OFFICE BEFORE THE MOST REVD. DESMOND MADU. WITNESSED BY PASTOR ANDREW OKONKWO, LAY-READER AND SECRETARY.

I, Adanna Matthew, female, 64years old. I am a member of the St. John Anglican Church in Ikenegbu, Owerri.

I am here to talk about my niece, Anjola Badmus who used to stay with me as far back as 1959. She was about nine years old when she came to live with me. Her mother had died when she was little and her father remarried to another woman in Western Nigeria where they lived. Her father was my late husband's younger brother.

In 1968, Anjola was engaged to be married to one young man by the name of Chinedu Okoroafor. I met this young man several times whenever he came to our place. I was then living at Shell Camp in Owerri. This youngman was well-behaved and responsible and clearly my niece Anjola liked him.

Their relationship was very serious and soon they started talking of getting married.

Like I said earlier this was in 1968 and the war had started then. I used to be a school teacher those days and Anjola lived with me and my two children, Chukwuemeka and Ujumadu. Unfortunately they are both late now (*sniff, sniff*).

There was a problem however that stopped them from going ahead with their marriage plans.

Chinedu's mother was opposed to the marriage and the young lovers told me about it when it looked like everything will fail.

I therefore offered to go to Chinedu's mother to see her and try to convince her to allow them to get married. She lives at Orogwe, which is about 6kms from Owerri.

I had never met her before that day when I went there to plead on behalf of my niece and Chinedu.

Everyone in the small town seemed to know her. When I eventually saw her, I knew why. She was a wealthy woman and even though her husband was late, she still managed his businesses successfully.

I told her my mission and after listening to me, she told me her side of the story and why she could not allow her son to marry Anjola. She said she had sworn to a deadly oath after her husband's death and if she violated it by allowing her son marry an outsider not from the village, she would either go mad or lose her life.

However, she also said it was a good thing that I had come. That she had a plan that I will have to help her execute to make everyone happy.

Her plan was that I will tell the young lovers that she had agreed to their wedding. That everything would proceed according to plan. But few weeks to the wedding day, Anjola would be made to fall sick and the illness would get worse. Finally, she will die a few days before the wedding.

In reality however, she would not die. Instead, I was supposed to give her something to eat to make her unconscious for days. Before the time she would wake up, we would have arranged with a friend of Nne Okoroafor in Calabar, who used to help the Biafran army smuggle in arms and supplies from foreign countries.

This man, whose name was Alfonso, would then take Anjola's still-unconscious body out of Nigeria and smuggle her to his own country. Nne Okoroafor said the man was from Angola. I don't know where that is, but they say it is very, very far.

Meanwhile, we would make arrangements for Anjola's burial here in Owerri, making sure that no one opened the coffin. Not even Chinedu would be allowed to look inside. So on the burial day, we would just be burying an empty coffin.

Everything worked according to our plan. I used some rat poison, *otapiapia* to make Anjola lose her senses. Nne Okoroafor gave them to me and she spent a lot of money to make everything work.

Please Father, forgive me. I agreed to this evil plan because she gave me a lot of money. You see Father, at that time, I had stopped teaching. Ojukwu had closed the schools and we were no more getting paid due to the war. I had no other income and I had no one to help me support my children. Father things were very, very difficult for me. Nne Okoroafor's money came at the right time for me and my children.

After the war about two years later, I tried to find this Alfonso man who took Anjola away but no one could trace him. I went to Calabar several times in search of him. Nne Okoroafor herself died during the war so I dare not tell anyone why I was looking for Alfonso. Because it was also during the war, there was a lot of confusion and many people lost families and property.

Father I ask for forgiveness of my sins everyday. I have suffered a lot for what I did to that poor girl. I feel I cheated not only her, but myself and I have paid dearly for it. She was an angel. A good child who trusted me with everything in her life. My children also adored her, Father. They never stopped asking me about her until they both lost their lives in a motor accident in 1977.

I have never known any peace since then Father. I am an old woman now and will leave this world soon. Please ask God for forgiveness for me Father. Please.

Below it was what looked more like a scrawl, but Dr Kalu guessed it would have been the woman's signature.

He shook his head several times, in bewilderment and wonder. Yes, he also knew Nne Okoroafor very well.

But why did she do this to her son? Her only child?

CHAPTER TWENTY EIGHT

'Oh my God! Oh my God!'

It was getting very cold as it always was these days, but the knowledge that this was probably her last night ever as a single woman, kept Angelou warm.

Maria and Big V had just left minutes ago, after coming home with her from work. As usual, the wedding tomorrow was all they spoke about and they were all cockahoot. Arranging, rearranging, fixing hairstyles, checking out dresses, shoes, bags and everything else under the sun.

It was a huge effort for Angelou to finally shoo them away, despite their protests. They actually suggested spending the night just in case she needed any help to get dressed the next day but she convinced them she would be okay and that they could pick her up in the morning.

Finally, they had calmed down enough to take her counsel and leave her in peace. But the signs of their presence were everywhere. Small white cartons of clothes, shoes, jewellery, new plates and cutlery littered the lounge-room. All the store labels she could think of were very well-represented in her house that night. Some opened. Others still sealed.

She set about tidying up a bit when she thought she heard a knock.

At this hour? It wasn't really late. Just gone past 7pm, but it was already pitch dark outside. Typical Johannesburg winter night.

Then the knock again.

"Yes? Who is that?", she enquired.

"It's me. I mean it's Dr Kalu. I have a message for you"

What? What did the man want at this hour?

"Em, can't it wait till tomorrow? I mean it's quite late now", she suggested.

"Com'on Madam. I'm not going to kidnap you or something. If it wasn't urgent, I won't be here at this time".

How she wished she had allowed her two friends to spend the night.

Against every ounce of will power she had, she reluctantly opened the door to let him in.

He was a big man in size. Standing in her living room now, he looked even more enormous.

"Sorry to bother you Madam. Something came up which I wanted you to help me with. It is kind of urgent", he explained haltingly.

"Okay, I was just surprised. I'm not used to receiving visitors at this time. Please have a seat".

"Oh thank you very much. I'll try to be quick. Oh", he broke off, looking around him, "you getting ready for a party or something?".

"No actually, I am getting married. That's why my friends came over to sort some new items out", she revealed to him. Hating him for putting her in a corner.

"You? Getting married? Why didn't anyone tell me before now? When?"

"Most people don't know yet. It is a very private thing. Actually it is tomorrow".

"Very interesting. I never knew you could still think of that at your age. Accept my congrats, ay?"

"Thank you very much", she responded between clenched lips.

"I just wonder who the very lucky man is", he asked with a wide but inquisitive grin.

"Well that is him over there", Angelou lavishly pointed at a portrait picture of her and Rupert sitting on the small coffee table. Eat your heart out, she wished him.

Dr Kalu sat transfixed for what seemed like an eternity. It was the same face in the other picture sent to him yesterday. Could it really be true?

His silence unsettled Angelou forcing her to ask: "Is everything alright Dr Kalu?"

He turned to face her, the smile and jesting now vanished from his face.

"What is his name? The young man?", he asked quietly. He had to be sure.

"It is Rupert. Rupert Mabizela. Do you know him?"

"No Madam, I don't but I don't think you can marry him".

"What?!", she almost screamed at him. How dare him come into her house and into her life and start telling her who to marry and who not.

"You can't marry him Madam. It is a long story, some of which you know and some you don't", Dr Kalu spoke slowly with deliberate care.

Now she really wished she had allowed the girls to stay. Who was this man and what did he want?

"Madam, I believe you used to be known as Anjola. Anjola Badmus"

If she had been slapped in the face, she wouldn't have reacted any worse.

Words failed her at that moment as she stared steadily at this hulking man sitting just 3-4 meters away from her. What did he want? Oh Lord, why now? Why?

"Madam, are you okay? Are you okay?", he enquired with obvious concern.

"I'm very okay. Yes, yes I used to be Anjola. That was in Nigeria a long time ago", she responded steadily, the first wave of shock having subsided. For a second, her face had been a mask of malice but now her composure had returned.

She had always suspected this man was trouble.

"What happened to you Anjola? Everyone thought you were dead? I even attended your funeral!"

"You cannot be serious! How would anyone think I was dead? Why?", she almost screamed at him.

For answer, he pulled out a copy of this morning's fax message from Reverend Madu and handed it over to her. She looked at him suspiciously before taking the sheets from his hands.

As she patiently read through them, her faced underwent several transformations. But she never for once stopped reading.

At last she put it down and buried her head in her hands.

"Oh my God!", she cried softly. "Oh my God!!".

Dr Kalu moved closer to hold her, but sensing his presence, she raised her head and fiercely ordered him, "Do not touch me, please. Let me be!".

Rebuffed, he kept his distance.

"Do you know the woman Ada? She claimed to be your auntie", he asked carefully.

"Yes she was. If I may ask also, what is your interest in all this?"

"Well, the truth is my first name is Nnanna and Chinedum was my friend".

Another deep shiver swept through her body like a tremor. That explained it. Yes, yes, it had to be him alright. Chinedum had mentioned him severally but she had never met him back then. Poor Chinedum.

"Where is he now? Where?", she almost begged him. Hating herself.

"Nedum died a long time ago. It was in a car accident. In case you wondered, he never married after you. He mourned you till his last breath. I must tell you also that during your mock burial staged by his mother, he created a huge scene. Jumping into the grave and asking them to bury him alive with you. There was a huge commotion that day Anjola. Everyone thought he was going to kill himself long after that day. He truly loved you. Oh he did".

By now tears were flowing freely on her beautiful face. The tears of many, many years ago that she had stubbornly suppressed. Tears of pain and loneliness and ignorance about what had happened to her. About the man that had loved her like his own skin. About the impossibility of their affair. Try as she may, she couldn't stem the flood that was washing down her face now.

"Please, I'm sorry Anjola. I'm sorry I had to bring you such sad news tonight. I never knew all these myself until last night", he managed to explain.

The woman sitting across from him dissolved into anguished weeping.

She cried out all her sadness and frustrations silently. Only her understood why she had to cry it all out now. Only her knew why she had to shed away all the pain of many agonizing years gone by.

CHAPTER TWENTY NINE

'This is my story / This is my song'

Inspite of her obvious torment, Dr Kalu knew the hardest part of this business still lay ahead.

He watched her calmly for about ten minutes after which he coughed gently as if to remind her that he was still here.

Still waiting.

"So Anjola, what happened to you after you were taken to Alfonso?", he asked her.

She sniffed several times, blowing her overflowing nose into a cream handkerchief. The emotions of the moment had certainly overwhelmed her.

"Who is Alfonso?", she asked from behind the handkerchief.

"The man your auntie took you to in Calabar. It is there in her confession".

"Oh, yes I remember someone that fits his description. I only came to my senses in Gabon. So they called the place. It was very dark and cold inside the boat I was with so many other men and women. They were refugees from the war... the Biafran war. Nobody was sure where we were going or where we were. But everyone kept asking this man Alfonso.

He wore a uniform like a soldier and carried two small guns. Other men who looked like soldiers also were receiving orders from him".

She stopped to wipe away more tears.

Having been warned earlier, Dr Kalu made no attempt to touch her.

"I had a severe headache and was also very hungry and thirsty at the same time. Some of the women had little children who were screaming at the top of their voices. It only made my headache worse. Also, it was very cold. Everyone was shaking. The men in uniform were smoking repeatedly and speaking a very strange language. Different from anything I had ever heard in Nigeria".

She paused to blow her nose inside the handkerchief again, eyeing the man sitting before her with some degree of suspicion.

"We were all anxious and frightened. No one was sure of where we were or where we were going. Some of the children who were not crying, were vomiting. A couple of the women were praying and asking God for help. Anyway, we remained in this state of uncertainty for many hours until it looked like dawn was breaking. All the time, the small boat was moving steadily as the men working with this Alfonso never stopped paddling with all their strength. Like I said earlier, when it looked like the darkness was lifting, the men stopped paddling and after speaking to Alfonso, one of them went into the water and started swimming. Everyone in the boat became suddenly silent. Meanwhile the boat had stopped".

"After a very long wait, the man returned with yet another man. By now, it was really light around us and we could all see that we were in the middle of an ocean. We could also hear faint noises in the distance as if people were shouting from afar. After a brief conversation with the men who just came from the water, Alfonso shouted something and the boat was slowly directed towards the sound of the faraway noises. Gradually, we were maneuvered to what turned out to be a small beach. More men appeared out of the bushes, all carrying guns and approached our boat. They looked menacing but also looked like they had been expecting us. Alfonso went down to meet them and they exchanged greetings in the strange language".

"At last, we were all ordered to disembark from the boat. Everyone was eager to get off; happy at least that we were finally on dry land. I surprised that by the time we all stood on the beach, we were over fifty, not including the little children. I could not believe that such a small boat could have contained us all. Anyway, the men took us further into this new place and we soon found ourselves in a small village. I suddenly realized that most of the people there were speaking Igbo. I was relieved. Even though I couldn't speak the language well, I understood enough of it to carry out some form of conversation. I could deduce from what they were saying that the war in Nigeria was getting worse and this place, that is the village, would soon be overflowing with more refugees. That was when I realized that we were all refugees from the war. The war of Biafra".

"I never for once stopped wondering about my Aunty Ada, Emeka and Uju. I also kept on wondering where was Chinedum? Why they were not all here? Why was I here alone? What about the wedding we were all planning and looking forward to? My head was filled with all these questions but no one could give me an answer. I approached a woman who was dressed like a sister, you know a nun at the church. I asked her if she knew Aunty Ada. She just shook her head silently, looking at me with sad eyes. I asked her also about Chinedum but she refused to say anything, shaking her head more vigorously again".

"Anyway, we were all in this village for about a week and some people with small radios kept on passing information to the rest of us about the war in Nigeria. I always wondered why they kept on referring to Nigeria as a distant place. One night I couldn't sleep. I thought I would go mad if someone did not give me an answer to my many questions. So I summoned up courage and approached one of the men with the radios and asked him where we were. He wasted no time in telling me that we were in Equitorial Guinea; trumpeting his superior knowledge. I asked him if it was far from Owerri and he just started laughing. After amusing himself for what seemed like a long time to me, he looked at me again and resumed laughing loudly. I couldn't understand what was so funny. Eventually he calmed down enough to tell me that Equitorial Guinea was very, very far from Owerri. Actually that we were no more in Nigeria. That we were the lucky ones who managed to escape the war in Nigeria. That the country we were now in, was our new home and we would be here until the war ended. I didn't know whether to cry or laugh".

"Later that day, some people in blue uniforms came and started distributing food in sealed packages. We had been in that village for over a week already and had been having only boiled cassava with fish. Everyone welcomed these new arrivals with their sweet-smelling food. The food tasted like those canned tins I used to go and buy at the supermarkets in Owerri. Eating them brought back stronger memories of home and out of desperation, I asked one of the men in blue uniforms if they were from Owerri. He smiled kindly and shook his head, replying in the strange language of the place we were staying. I used my hands to tell him I couldn't understand. He made a sign to say he was going away; that I should wait. True to his words, he came back with another woman, who was about 50years old. This woman explained to me that they were volunteer workers, looking after refugees. I asked her all the questions that had occupied my mind for days, but she only managed to tell me that truly we were in Equitorial Guinea and the government there was looking after us until the end of the war. I asked her where exactly was Equitorial Guinea and she said it was three days' journey by sea from Nigeria. I couldn't believe I had been in that boat for three days. Why did I only wake up on the last day? The woman said there were several other refugees like that also from Nigeria in many locations in the country and that they still expected more".

"I never saw the woman again because about a week later, Alfonso appeared in the village, this time with more people who looked like they were from the war in Nigeria. They all looked frightened and reminded me of my group when we first arrived. To my surprise, I was approached by one of the men I had seen with Alfonso in the boat. He came to me and asked me stand up and come with him. I obeyed and after walking for a few minutes, we came to a hut. He went in first and after a few minutes, came out, beckoning me to go in. I went in with a lot of fear. Inside, Alfonso was sitting alone, counting what looked like currency notes from different countries. He motioned me to sit on a high chair near the bed he was sitting on. I didn't know what to expect and was too afraid to ask".

"After a longtime, he asked me if I was Angelou? I said yes, because I was too afraid to correct him. Too afraid to insist that I was Anjola. He said he had been instructed to bring me here to save me from the war in Nigeria. That all my family members were in hiding in Nigeria but I was lucky to be able to escape with my life and be on the boat that brought me here. He said he was going to help me start a new life and become a pride to my family. His English was very strange and sometimes, I couldn't understand very well what he meant. He talked about a boat; another boat; he talked about travelling; about a country called Angola; about me going with the boat. I just sat there, too frightened to express myself. Even though he spoke to me with some respect and never raised his voice, my experiences over the past weeks had put too much fear of the unknown into me. Eventually, he asked me if I understood him. I quickly shook my head and hurriedly left his presence, escorted by one of his men".

All the time we were in this camp, I found it hard to eat properly. My stomach rejected most of the food given me and I was constantly vomiting. One of the people in blue uniform gave me some white tablets but it didn't help much. I lost a lot of weight and felt sick a lot. It really confused me because I never remembered ever being sick".

Suddenly a phone started ringing somewhere in the house. It was in her bedroom.

Excusing herself, Angelou stood up and went into her room. The call was from Maria, who wanted to know the colour of hat they all agreed to put on for the next day. Angelou confirmed that they had all agreed on pink.

"Are you okay Angel? You sound like you've been crying", her friend enquired.

"Crying over what? Look you are just imagining too much. C'mon go to sleep or you'll be too tired tomorrow", Angelou fended her off, trying her best to keep her voice from shaking.

"Ok, if you say so. I'll see you in the morning, ay?"

"Sure, I'll be here waiting for you".

She hung up carefully, breathing slowly.

Walking back into the lounge room, she got herself a cup of water and again sat down before her visitor who hadn't moved all the while.

CHAPTER THIRTY

Oh my home, oh my home, when shall I see my home?/
when shall I see my native land?

By now Angelou had regained a lot of her usual composure.

She spoke steadily now, looking straight at the wall behind the man before her. Her mind replaying all the harrowing experience of decades back as if they had happened yesterday.

"So that was how I left Nigeria. Obviously I was unconscious and only woke up on the boat. Till this day, I have no idea how I got on the boat. However, the condition in the camp was not so bad. The people in blue uniform who I later learned were from the UN, did their best for us. They provided clothes, food, blankets and even books. I cherished the books a lot because it afforded me the chance to pass the time. I also learnt more about Equitorial Guinea; that it was a small, Portuguese-speaking place. Eventually, I learnt it was the language I had heard Alfonso speaking."

"As for Alfonso, he hardly stayed there. We only saw him whenever a new batch of refugees arrived. I prayed everyday secretly that each new batch would include Aunty Ada, or the two children, or my beloved Chinedum, or just anyone from my school. Anybody who knew someone from

Owerri. Of course none of them came with the new arrivals. I even started asking the new people if they knew any of my family. Since most of them were Igbos, I was hopeful someone would at least know my family".

"None of them did. Infact hardly any of them was from Owerri. Almost all of them were from Port Harcourt, or Calabar or Aba. A few said they came from Onitsha. My high hopes which went up every time a new batch was coming, always ended up dashed because no one knew my people. I cried a lot then but when I also listened to the various stories of narrow-escape and suffering shared by the people in the camp, I eventually realized how lucky I was to even be alive. To have come out of the war alive."

"A common thought among everyone in the camp then, was how little they all realized that the Biafrans were losing the war. Everyone always said they believed Ojukwu and the stories of heroic gallantry of Biafran soldiers. Until of course they woke up one morning to find Nigerian soldiers on their streets, forcing them into an inevitable and shameful surrender. In my heart, I realized also that no one around me then in Owerri thought the war was being lost".

All along, Dr. Kalu kept shaking his head, recollecting his own bitter experiences at that time, but preferring to stay silent until he heard this woman out.

"Anyway, I never saw anyone I knew until one morning, about two months after we had been in the camp, I was asked to go before Alfonso again. This time, he looked much-less frightening for no apparent reason. He greeted me in his strange accent and told me to get ready. That the boat he told me about the last time, would be leaving in two hours and I had to be on it. I was now much more bolder and told me I wanted to go back to Nigeria. He looked at me as if I was mad and said point blankly that it was impossible. That the war still on and that his job was to bring people out of Nigeria, and not take them in. That in my case, he was directed to take me to a safer place than where I was now. That I would be well-looked after there. That the new place was actually his home country. He mentioned Angola, but since I had never heard the name before, it made absolutely no meaning to me. When I asked him who instructed him to take me, he only said the person paid good money and he had to fulfill his part of the bargain. That I should be grateful that I had people who cared for me as to want to save my life at such great expense".

"His words made me say silent prayer-after-prayer for Aunty Ada, believing it was her who had put me on the boat to save me from the war. Nonetheless, minutes later, I was led along with about four other people, all women onto a small boat. This boat was pushed out to sea by Alfonso's men who climbed onto it and rowed out. At first I thought this was our transportation to Angola but after about an hour, we saw a huge, grey ship. The sort I had only ever seen in picture books. It was this ship that we eventually boarded".

"On the ship, I was given a small room to share with a woman who spoke Alfonso's language, but understood English as well. She said she was a cook and tried to make me comfortable. I had no idea where Angola was and asked her. I almost fainted when she told me it was three weeks journey. I never in my wildest imagination thought it was that far".

"Actually, the trip lasted a little over a month. I was sick for most of it and had little recollection of what happened on the ship. It turned out to be a ship used for carrying palm oil and everywhere the smell of it hung on the ship.

But the cook was heaven-sent. She looked after me and brought me meals most of the time because I was too sick to even leave the room. I found out that her name was Martha because I often heard people banging on the door and calling her. She was my guardian angel on that ship and if not for her, I doubt if I would have come out of it alive. I never again saw the other four people I left the camp with".

"Like I said, the journey lasted over a month. Eventually, we were told to prepare to disembark because we had arrived. It was Martha who came and told me one morning as I sat on my bunk, my eyes swimming from nausea. I was so frail and fragile I was sure I would fall over if I tried to stand up".

"Martha it was who carried me on her back like a child as we came off the ship. Outside was very hot. Hotter than I had known in my life. Ahead of me, I could see people mostly covered in white. I asked Martha feebly if this was Angola. She said she wasn't sure, but that the name of the place was Swakopmund. Since I was too weak to even hear properly, I assumed she said Angola. Actually the people I thought were dressed in white clothes from the ship, were white people. I had never seen so many of them at one place in all my life and asked Martha again if Angola was full of white people. I could not remember her answer because I soon fell asleep, unaware of where I was or whom I was with."

"I must have slept for a long time because when I woke up, I was hot and sweating like a chicken in an oven. I also found myself in a large, bright room in front of a black and white television set. On the screen was yet another white woman speaking in a language very different from even Alfonso's and behind her was a banner that attracted my attention. It read: **Namibia Television**. It didn't make any sense but I was still very weak. Unknown to me however, the banner was very accurate. I had landed in Namibia. Not Angola".

CHAPTER THIRTY ONE

Man is nothing without hope

"I must have drifted off to sleep again because suddenly I realized there were many people in the room all talking loudly at the same time. I managed to open my eyes and saw many boys sitting around yelling at the tv. From where I lay it was obvious that there was something interesting them on the tv, which brought about the raised voices. Then almost as soon as I opened my eyes, I saw to my great relief, Martha bursting into the room".

"She spoke harshly and angrily at all the boys and they all quietly stood up and left the room. When the last of them had left, she switched off the tv and came over to me. She asked me how I was and if I wanted to eat. Though I was hungry, my immediate need was to know exactly where I was. She told me it was truly a country called Namibia, in a small town by name Swakopmund. She went on to tell me about the place. That it was by the sea and that when I had enough strength, they planned to take me to another place on the coast called Walvis Bay, from where I was expected to be given fake papers to cross the border into a bigger country called South Africa. When I asked her why I had to be smuggled to this bigger, strange place, she only said it was the orders given to them by Alfonso".

"To cut a long story short, I was in this place for about a week after which my health improved considerably. One night, Martha took me to a small shopped owned by some white people and bought me new clothes, shoes and other items. She was really a good woman and helped me to the best of her ability".

"By now I had given up hope of ever seeing anyone from my family or Owerri and though it bothered me a lot, I still felt gratitude to Aunty Ada for helping me escape the war. By the time I was taken in a big truck to Walvis Bay, my state of mind had improved. One thing kept bothering me though and it was that I was growing big around the middle. I became tired easily and often woke up with a strong urge to vomit. This strange feeling bothered me but I was also reluctant to tell anyone".

"At Walvis Bay, I was surprised to see that most of the people there spoke English. A very dark-skinned man with big earrings received me asking if I was Angelou. I replied in the affirmative and followed him to what looked like a shop. There, he gave me some papers which to my surprise had my name on it but they added a strange one, Fanteni as my surname. I told him what the papers were for. He explained impatiently that it was my pass to enter into South Africa and that he was going to take me across the border that night. I asked him how far the journey would be and he said it was just an hour's trip".

"Contrary to what he said though, the journey lasted throughout the night. I fell asleep through most of it though and only woke up when the sun started beating down on me at the back of the truck where I was hidden. Soon after I woke up, the truck rolled into a small town and stopped.

The man with big earrings, who I never knew his name, came round to meet me and asked me to climb down. I asked him when we would get to South Africa but to my surprise, he said we were already there. That we crossed the border at night and we had arrived at a place called Prieska".

"Like I said, he never spoke much. Instead he took my small bag in his hand and grabbed me by the other. He was rough and unfriendly. Eventually, after walking through some streets, he knocked on a gate. A voice spoke through a small wire-mesh opening and he replied the voice. Soon, the gate opened and we went into the house. Inside, he spoke some very strange language to a half-white, half-black skinny lady who looked at me suspiciously and nodded at the man. Soon the man handed over my bag to the lady and asked me to go with her. After he left, the lady took me into a kitchen and asked if I spoke English. She musn't have been expecting me to yes, but when I did, she looked me over again this time more curiously."

Angelou paused to drink some more water, still not caring to offer her late-night visitor anything.

"It was in this house that I discovered I was pregnant. I came to that reluctant conclusion that night when I felt something move continuously inside my stomach. I approached the woman, who said her name was Charmaine and told her how I felt. She initially looked angry but later told me she would call someone to come and check me. That someone came in the form of an old white man with big glasses. He asked me to lie on a flat table and moved his ancient fingers all over my stomach. I was embarrassed having to lift up my dress in front of strangers, but they both didn't seem to care".

"After touching my stomach and thighs to his satisfaction, the man straightened up and spoke quietly to

Charmaine, who responded even more quietly. She then turned to me and announced that I was seven months pregnant. I couldn't believe my ears. The shock almost made me want to start crying allover again. I managed to calm down though and thought sadly of Chinedum. Of course it had to be him. But we had only done it once and he had assured me that nothing would happen after. I was confused, sad, depressed".

CHAPTER THIRTY TWO

And a man's foes.....shall be his own household

"Charmaine later explained to me that she knew a place where they could take out the child if I didn't want it. I didn't know what to say to her. All her questions about me and why I left Nigeria I answered truthfully and she said they all had heard about the war in my country. She turned out to actually be a good companion, though she was no Martha. I also noticed that she drank heavily and was often in a mood after having some alcohol. She was actually not the owner of the house. She said it belonged to her husband, whom she also said traveled a lot and sometimes went away for weeks. She equally told me that she was childless and suspected that her husband had other women elsewhere".

"I had been in the house for almost three weeks when the husband came in one afternoon. He was also half-black and half-white like Charmaine and told me that he had been expecting me long, long ago from Angola. He asked if Alfonso was my uncle, to which I told him I knew absolutely nothing of Alfonso. He just smiled and told me that on his next trip to the Eastern Cape, I would be going with him. When I asked him what for, he replied that I had to go to school there. That it had all been paid for by Alfonso. I didn't know what to say".

"Unfortunately after two days I started feeling painful pangs in my stomach at night. I woke up sweating and screaming, which attracted Charmaine. She looked drunk as she swayed unsteadily in front of me but I needed help and didn't care who turned up at that moment. I was bundled onto what must be a donkey cart and taken somewhere out of the house. A million darts of pain were ravaging all of my body and I just screamed and screamed till my voice vanished. All the time, I felt a shape coming out of my legs bit by bit. I guessed it was the child coming but the pain was just unbearable".

"I must have passed out because eventually, I woke up in a large room surrounded by strange people all lying on beds. It must have been a hospital surely. I couldn't talk even though I was dying to ask someone all manner of questions. Soon a white-clothed black woman walked past and I raised my hand to draw her attention. She saw me but kept going. Soon, she came back with three people among whom was Charmaine".

"She came and sat by my bed, talking softly to me all the time. She said I had fainted and they had had to carry me inside and placed me here. She kept asking if I wanted anything, repeatedly placing a finger on my lips to indicate that I shouldn't talk. I wasn't sure if I really could talk, but I sure wanted to say something. To ask the one question that was burning through my brain. Charmaine kept a conversation going between her, myself and the two other people who looked like hospital staff. Eventually, they all left and I must have drifted off to sleep again".

"When I woke up, I was surprised to find that I was back in my bed, in the house. I was alone. This time I was determined to find an answer to the only question gnawing at my senses. I pushed myself off the bed and was staggering towards the door, when it swung open and Charmaine walked in with a tray of hot food in her hands. She grabbed me and led me gingerly back to the bed, softly rebuking me for my effort. I allowed myself to be led back to the bed where I summoned enough strength to tell her that I wanted to see the child. She first let out a deep sigh, before averting her eyes to the ground and told me slowly that there was no child. That I had lost it. That it had come out stillborn. I held her by the arm, too weak to say anything else except cry more tears of despair and anguish".

"Eventually, I regained my strength and recovered from all the trauma. Charmaine actually warmed up to me and tried her utmost to make me overcome the loss of the child. She comforted me over and over, telling me that the people at the hospital said it was the severe stress and discomfort of my difficult travel from Nigeria over many months that affected the child. I accepted this as a tangible reason and succumbed to fate. Painful though it was that the last fragment of Chinedum had been cruelly snatched away from me by the cold hands of death".

"I soon returned back to full health and left Prieska for Eastern Cape to begin my education at Fort Hare in the small town of Alice under the name Angelou Fanteni. I had grown up rapidly courtesy of all the harrowing experiences that befell me over the past ten months. No single day passed by without me thinking of my family back home and what could have become of them. I prayed for their safety and well-being, believing that no matter how long it took, I would see them again one day. I never stopped praying specially for Aunty Ada in the belief that she had spent everything she had to take me out

Emma Nwaneri

of harm's way by bringing me to South Africa. I never stopped thinking of Chinedum also because in this case, as they always say, out of sight was never out of mind. That was my story, doctor".

CHAPTER THIRTY THREE

Ye shall know the truth and the truth shall set ye free

Dr Kalu sat there. He had sat still for the over one hour it had taken Angelou to narrate her astonishing story. As she had spoken, many jigsaws that had occupied his mind started unraveling one after the other.

"I hope you are satisfied now", Angelou asked him sarcastically. Regarding him as a caged animal would regard his captor. The fact that it was him of all people that she had to unburden her past to, riled her to the bones.

"I have to admit that your experience was really unpleasant. I mean how could anyone go through what you experienced and still not be bitter?", he asked rhetorically.

"Bitter against who? Or against what?", it was her turn to ask.

"Bitter against the people that made you suffer like that. Risking your life over all that distance. Travelling in unsafe boats with unknown people through unknown places. I mean anything could have gone wrong. You could have been kidnapped, or killed or raped as a young girl. Anything at all. How could you not be bitter?"

"Who was I to be bitter against? Like I told you, I believed it was Aunty Ada who arranged it all to save me from the war. It was only this night that you brought her confession that I only knew the truth", said Angelou.

"And that is not the only truth. There are still a couple more things you need to know. Remember I told you at the start that you cannot marry this young man. Rupert is it?"

Angelou froze. Yes, he had mentioned it but...

"You cannot marry him Anjola. He is your son. Your child".

She wasn't sure she had heard him right.

Dr Kalu's eyes were avoiding hers. Reminding her of Charmaine many, many years back.

"What do you mean, please?", she asked quietly, a deep fear gathering in her stomach.

This time he looked up. Fixing his eyes on her.

"Anjola, Rupert is your son. The child you were told died at birth in that village. You cannot marry him".

At first, he thought she would collapse or do something rash. But she sat there as if struck by lightning. But her face remained a study in anguish.

"How do you know this? You haven't even met him?", she parried hopefully.

"No I haven't, but I've met his father. Or so-called father", while speaking he pulled out the old picture in his pocket and handed it to a trembling Angelou.

Reluctantly, as if it was dangerous, she took it gingerly and looked at it.

It must have been taken about fifteen years back but there was no mistaking a young Rupert standing between two older couple. The man was black, middle-aged; of hefty build but it was the skinny woman on his right that Angelou starred and starred at. She knew her. She would know her anywhere.

"Who are these people? What is going on? I...I know the woman. That is Charmaine I just told you about!", she asked as a numb, chilly feeling crept up her spine.

"Yes it is Charmaine. Yes of course that is Rupert in the middle and the man is his so-called father. But you see, Rupert must have told you he grew up in Kimberley. It isn't very far from Prieska which was where you stayed with Charmaine. She took the baby from you at childbirth and told you that he died. Of course he didn't. I did some research since I came here and got in touch with a colleague at Springbok, who works with the museum there. He often visits Nigeria for seminars and things like that. He traced Rupert's so-called father to Kimberley and managed to convince him to let him have this picture. Rupert's so-called father is actually an older brother to Charmaine. She brought Rupert there after she stole her from you. Remember she told you she was childless, which was true. She couldn't keep him with her at Prieska because it was a very small town and everyone knew she had no child. How would she explain the sudden appearance of this new baby?".

Dr Kalu halted to consider his lone audience's reaction. So far, there was none as she just sat mute, staring into the picture in her hand with glazed eyes.

"So she took your baby to her brother at Kimberley who also was childless and lived alone. But for a man to claim a child as it's own wasn't as difficult unlike a woman. He raised the child and Charmaine often came regularly to visit. It must have been during one of those visits that the picture was taken. Charmaine, I gathered, later left her husband and moved to North West, somewhere around Mafikeng in search of work. She was last known to have been working as a waitress around the squatter camps where miners lived.

For the past ten or so years, no one has heard of her, so she is presumed dead. Rupert's so-called dad, Sipho Mabizela told my friend that his sister lived a hard, rough life. Always moving from men to men. Most of them she picked up at bars and drinking spots".

Angelou still sat still. Her eyes boring into the picture as if willing all the people in it to come out and tell her all this was not true. But deep down, she knew the whole truth about the missing punctuations of her life had just been uncovered. A truth she had never imagined existed.

"So you see Anjola", he summarized regretfully, "you cannot marry him. He's your son. Your stolen child".

CHAPTER THIRTY FOUR

The first law of nature is always self-preservation

As much as she wanted this night to end and daylight come.

As much as she wanted daylight to arrive and turn all this into one big, bad dream.

As much as she kept telling herself that this was just a nightmare that would evaporate at the first light of dawn.

As much as she sat there, pretending that all of this was really not happening; she also felt a stronger, more-powerful conviction that everything was true.

So it had all come down to this. To this stark revelation. All she had hoped and prayed for. Just on the eve of fulfillment. At the doorstep of realization. At the point of her final accomplishment, the door of defeat had to be slammed in her face.

Though she didn't look it, she felt crushed.

The man had to be saying the truth. His fatal disclosures, though innocently done, had driven home the bare facts of her situation. It had unearthened who she really was. What she had been and where she now belonged. Though she had been guiltless in all the contending coincidences that had converged to now conspire against her, she still felt cheated.

Now really, she had reason to be bitter.

She had suspected somewhere in the back of her mind that Rupert had been too good to be true. Too perfect for her.

All the similarities with Chinedum that she noticed in him, had actually all been inherited. The boy was simply reflecting his father. The father he never knew. The man cruelly snatched away from her. The man that remained an immortal link between them both. Who made it possible for her and the boy to maintain an everlasting umbilical bond.

The same man whose role in both she and the boy's life would make their togetherness impossible.

She had wondered about his looks. She had wondered about his good manners. She had wondered about his height. More poignantly, she had wondered about his habit of lip-chewing. Everything bore too much resemblance with Chinedum. Sometimes when they were together, she had felt it was her late lover sitting there.

Was that why she initially harboured motherly tendencies towards the boy? So they had been correct feelings.

The boy was a copy of his father in all things physical and mental. Initially, she had attributed this to her still, deep attachment to Chinedum. She had considered telling Maria and Vivian, but then again they would have dismissed it all as her hanging on to the past. But would they?

As she sat there, she recollected so many scenes and events from her past. Everything seemed to have been building up to this night. This cursed night. This night of all nights. The eve of her wedding.

Dr Kalu was talking again.

"Are you okay Anjola?".

She hated him even more for using her real name. As if determined to stamp her past into the present. The damned man.

"So what are you going to do now?", he asked still.

"I have to think. I have to see Rupert. I think it's late already tonight. Don't you think it's time you started going?", she confronted him. Her tormentor.

"Em, I was thinking, you don't have to cancel the wedding", he suggested.

"What on earth do you mean? I just discovered that he is my son for God's sake!", she almost screamed at him.

"Yes I know, but the wedding can still go ahead. You know", he now spoke rapidly. "You can still be married tomorrow as you planned".

When she didn't say anything, just starring at him in mock horror, he ploughed on.

"I see you really wanted to be married and I also want it to come to pass for you. You see, I'm also single. I'm divorced. It was a long time ago. But you know I also like you Anjola. I tried my best to make you know that since I came here but you always avoided me. I wanted to at least let you know my feelings for you. You are a beautiful woman my dear. You are smart. You are well-respected here also. You are everything I want in a woman Anjola. I will be the best husband for you. I will make you the happiest woman. No one else has to know about Rupert. That he is your son and you almost got married to him. You owe only him an explanation. It will be our secret together. The three of us. You can tell him that at your age, you suddenly felt too old to be married to him. I know it is very sudden but he will understand. He is still young....he will find a girl his age with time. Please let's consider this. I like you very much Anjola. I've not been myself since that night I set eyes on you in the hall. I knew you were the woman for me. Please my dear. Please say yes. Please!", he suddenly went down on his knees.

Angelou looked at him as if he had suddenly gone mad.

His words had sounded like barbs of arrow striking at her heart. Could he be serious? Did he realize what he was saying? So far as she could see, the man wasn't drunk. Just plain selfish.

Her marry him? Was that why he had taken it upon himself to dig into her past? To hold her to ransom like this?

Her evening had surely been a complete package.

A night to remember for the rest of her life. If she still had any.

CHAPTER THIRTY FIVE

A dinner with the devil will always leave your stomach empty

"I will think about it", she heard herself say.

"Are you serious?", he asked. Elation streaming through his body.

"Yes, I will think about it. The revelations this night have been a big shock and I must say it is also a setback but your suggestion is quite thoughtful. Please give me a few days to think about it. I can't decide now. We'll have to cancel the wedding tomorrow".

Did she hear him heave a sigh of relief? She was sure she did because immediately, he leapt to his feet with a mild look of triumph on his face.

She glanced at the clock and to her surprise, it was approaching 11pm. The several revelations of her past had taken up half of the night.

"Em, I will have to go now, so when can I expect to hear from you my dear?", he asked hopefully.

She resented him calling her 'my dear'. This bearer of ill-tidings. This heartless opportunist.

She focused her tired eyes on him. Regarding him comprehensively for the first time since the past three hours they had been in the room together.

"I said give me a few days. I will get in touch. I may have to come to your office, or better still your house. I believe it is on the campus?", she enquired, feigning interest.

"No, I still stay at the school quarters in town. It is close to Ellis Park".

"Oh I do remember. I will get in touch, ok. Before you go, can you do me a small favour?", she asked.

"Oh yes, of course whatever you want my dear".

There he goes again. The shameless shylock.

"Yes. I just wanted you to promise to keep all this quiet. I will want to talk with Rupert first and break the news to him. Like you said, we can keep it secret between us three. I hope you can be trusted to maintain your silence", she inquired of him.

"Of course my dear, you can trust me. No one will hear of all this".

"Especially Rupert, please...he's my primary concern. I will want him to hear it from me first", she was almost pleading.

"I fully understand. It will all be a huge shock to him and no one can say how it may affect him. I agree with you", he promised, smiling at the same time.

Now she had squeezed that concession from him, she strode towards the door to open it and usher him out.

As he passed by her on his way out, he tried to catch her eyes.

But she wasn't giving him that pleasure.

All of her revolted at his presence. She knew she would rather drop dead than be seen with or touched by this man. This snake who had spent so much time and resource unearthing her past only to use it against her at her most vulnerable moment.

This so-called friend of Chinedum's who was indeed a chameleon. A masquerade. Prowling and watching her every step. Waiting for his chance to pounce.

She already had her answer to his bizarre request. But he would find out the same heartbroken way she had been denied of her dream.

She shut the door after him and bolted it firmly.

CHAPTER THIRTY SIX

The angel of death has no favourite person

Even before the 'evil doctor' had departed, she had reached her decision.

It was the only way. Nothing else could atone for the feeling of injustice she felt right now. The feeling of being cheated.

Not only had she been wronged both by people she trusted and by fate, innocent Rupert had also been dragged into a destructive web of deceit. Of which she had played a major, though unconscious part.

There had to be only one way to resolve it and forever wipe away the stigma bound to follow her for the rest of her existence.

She only felt sorry for him. Very sorry indeed.

Sorry that he had been a victim of a complex interplay of circumstances that would haunt him as long as he lived. Forces he had absolutely no say about.

If she had her way, he would never, ever hear the heart-wrenching stories she had both narrated and heard tonight. If only she had the power.

All of her life, she had been like a wandering spirit. In search of something she knew not. Seeking an explanation for who she was. Why she was what she was? Where she was headed to? What had destiny kept in store for her? Why the dearest people to her had cast her adrift without a second thought? Why she couldn't just live a normal life like everyone else?

And she found the answers. She found them at last on this night. An incredible night of astonishing truths.

Try as she may, she found it hard to blame anyone. Not Aunty Ada. Not Charmaine. Not even Nne Okoroafor. There was nothing to gain from pointing fingers.

Whatever their separate intentions had been, they had all helped her in finding answers to her life. They had all, in their disconnected deeds, helped her to discover herself. To leave an impression on the tracks of an era. She had been like a plant without roots. Uprooted from somewhere unknown and transplanted to a more-remote place and given little chance of survival.

But survive she had. She had overcome all the complications of her life to survive. She had outlasted. She had endured. Even excelled. As HOD in an institution like Johannesburg university, achievements don't come any cheaper. She had fought a good fight.

But like a plant also, its glory lay in its flower. Soon after it would wither and die away quietly. She was convinced that her time had come.

She walked straight to the kitchen cabinet where she normally kept all the cleaning items. She had separated it from her medicine compartment because, who knows it might contaminate the rest of the life-saving medications.

It was hidden at the back but after a few seconds probing with her right hand, she found it. The small, yellow bottle. It was still sealed since that day she got it to deal with the problem of rodents that sometimes foraged in her kitchen at night.

She shook it. Unscrewed it and poured a sizeable portion of the dark liquid down her throat. It wasn't as bitter as she thought. It was all done without hesitation. She was convinced it was the only way.

Quickly, she strolled back into the lounge-room for one last look. Nothing seemed out of place. She then proceeded to her bedroom and lay down on the huge, eiderdown covering her bed.

A kind of peace descended on her. The type the Bible described as passing all understanding.

Lord have mercy on me, she prayed silently. Please, please have mercy on me.

Suddenly she thought of her father. He rarely entered her consciousness, but this night he was imprinted strongly in it. She had always wondered why he never had any affection for her. She had always questioned why he never bothered to come visit her since she left Sabo and came to Aunty Ada's place at Owerri.

Ah Aunty Ada! She remembered all their small talk and shared jokes and joint deliberations together to solve one household problem or the other. Having had no recollection of her own mother, she had adopted the older woman as her parent. She had loved and worshipped and respected and adored her.

Aunty Ada was not evil, despite her confession she had read just hours ago. She had no doubts about that in her heart. She had been under pressure; that she believed. After all she did it because, *"I had no one to help me support my children...things were very, very difficult for me"*.

Lying there all alone in the house, she forgave the older woman unreservedly. She would always, always be her Aunty Ada. Till death did them part.

A sharp pain suddenly pierced her body, forcing her to grip her stomach tightly. Almost immediately, she was sweating and freezing at the same time. She knew it had begun.

Then again, she saw several faces in what looked like a crowd. She recognised some of the faces like Uju. Like Emeka. Like Nne Okoroafor. Like Charmaine. They were all smiling at her. Then she noticed another very familiar shape. It was a man but his back was turned to her. She wanted to run and touch him but the more she tried, the more he moved further from her. She still kept on, as more violent pain racked her body and spread rapidly like lava.

Somehow, she felt very strongly that if she managed to reach the figure of the man running away from her, all would be okay. So she persisted and kept up the chase. But it became harder and harder as more pain engulfed her body, making it contract and expand simultaneously.

She noticed that the room was swimming before her. Her focus was getting blurred. Things were out of order all around her. She imagined all the many items in the room suddenly rising off the ground and floating around in the air. Disorientated, she felt like crying out but no sound issued from her quivering lips.

Suddenly the man running away from her stopped and turned round. He was also smiling. A baleful smile. He stretched out his hands to her. She reached out to touch him and as she fell, stumbling into his hands, she at that last instant realized it was Chinedum.

That earlier, wonderful peace she had felt returned to envelope her for the final time.

CHAPTER THIRTY SEVEN

'Weep not child; weep not my darling. With these kisses let me dry your tears'
– Ngugi Wa Thiongo

It was Maria that found her first in the morning.

She had called her on the phone to wish her a happy married day, but Angelou wasn't picking her calls.

Unperturbed, she had dressed up as they had all agreed and headed for the bride's home to make sure she beat Vivian or anyone else to the place.

Instead, after repeatedly banging on the front door without getting any response, she had sneaked round to the back and peered through her friend's shut bedroom window. Peering inside, she had glimpsed Angelou lying sprawled out on her bed. Her repeated knocking on the glass window failed to rouse her, which was what triggered panic in her.

She immediately called Vivian's phone and asked her to come over as soon as she could. She still kept on banging on her friend's bedroom window, hoping against all odds that she would finally come out of her sleep and allow her in.

Vivian soon arrived and both now non-plussed, took turns in trying to arouse Angelou with increased shouts and thumping on the window pane.

A male gardener working in the next compound heard all the noise and joined them. With his help, they managed to prise the bedroom window open. The man was small in size, so he easily squeezed through the window and went into the room.

He then went round and opened the front door for the two panic-stricken women, who looked very comical all dressed-up in bright attires and high heels.

They all descended on Angelou's prostrate form and almost immediately realised that it was cold and lifeless.

"Oh my God, what on earth could have happened to Angel?", Maria asked in genuine horror.

"Oh God! Oh God!", Vivian just repeated senselessly.

It was the gardener who found the small yellow bottle lying by the foot of the bed. He held it up for the two women to read the name, Codicine, boldly printed on the side.

They all knew what it was. It was actually a pesticide, containing large amounts of the deadly substance organophosphate and turpentine. Any human consumption of it was very fatal.

"Why did she have to do this?! Oh goodness, why did she have to poison herself?!", Mariam wailed rhetorically on the verge of a deluge of tears.

"On the morning of her wedding of all days?", Vivian threw in her own question.

"I sensed she had been crying last night when I called her on the phone! I knew something was wrong!!", Maria recollected tearily.

What they were witnessing was too tragic to understand. Too terrible to make any sense of. They just sat huddled together; weeping and grieving helplessly. Unconsolably.

It was the gardener again that found the confession note. Being unable to read and write, he brought it to the weeping women who sat disconsolately on the bedroom floor pouring out their grief.

Vivian took it with trembling fingers and held it out for Maria to also read amidst teary eyes.

It was on the second reading that its contents finally made some meaning.

"Oh God! Why? Why? Why?!", Vivian repeated senselessly

They both knew the story of Angelou's flight from Nigeria during the war over there, but never had any of them thought it was the handiwork of some people with a sinister motive.

The confession letter of Aunty Ada was quite revealing, but definitely not enough reason for Angelou to take her own life. There had to be something else.

At the top of the letter, there was a faint telephone number. Or was it a fax number?

Amidst severe hiccups and tears, Vivian, who was the better-composed of the two, wrote down the number and made a mental note to check it with a friend who worked with Telkom.

From hitherto planning a dream wedding, both women found themselves inadvertently involved in the unpleasant and gloomy task of organizing their beloved friend's funeral.

Unknown to them both, a similar scenario had occurred over three decades ago faraway in the deep, remote forests of Eastern Nigeria. At that time, it had been a make-believe burial.

This time however, it would be for real. The only eerie similarity between three decades ago and the present, being the identity of the corpse meant for both burials.

Anjola and Angelou.

CHAPTER THIRTY EIGHT

What I have done is yours; what I have to do is yours; being part in all I have, devoted yours – William Shakespeare

Scientists believe it takes about 100 tears to fill a teaspoon. According to their calculation, all human beings therefore cry about 1,850,000million tears in an entire lifetime.

Between the two of them, Vivian and Maria exhausted their life time allocation of tears on the morning of the funeral.

The sudden occurrence and nature of their friend's demise had shocked them both to the depths of their marrows. It was like nothing they had ever witnessed before in both their lives.

It didn't make sense to them.

Whatever it was that was bothering her, or had led her to cut short her own life, could have been talked over among them all. Whatever it was could surely not be too much for them all to work out some solution.

Why did she have to do it? Why on the eve of her wedding? Had she changed her mind about it? Or was it Rupert who grew cold feet at the last moment?

But he was as shocked and heartbroken as them both and had cried like a baby when he arrived at her house in response to their frantic summons.

It just didn't make sense to them that their beloved Angel had even considered a thing as drastic as suicide.

Was she really gone? Gone forever and ever out of their lives?

Maria and Vivian were inconsolable amidst the small group that gathered three days later to give Angelou a quiet but fitting burial.

Everyone gathered there was shaken by the sudden, unexpected demise of this fine woman. She had been seen as icon. To many more, she was an epitome of everything noble and admirable.

In his requiem by her graveside, Professor Nomvete described her as success personified. He told the mourners gathered there that, "If you lose wealth, you've lost nothing. If you lose your health, you may have lost something. If you lose integrity, you've lost everything. Angelou Fanteni will never be lost to anything in our minds".

Maria's speech was however the one that resonated most with everyone in attendance there. She said: "The world now is filled with bigger houses but lonelier people; more money, less happiness; more knowledge, less commonsense; advanced medicine but more sick people; greater religions but more ungodliness. In the midst of all these, a woman like Angelou came to show us that men and women are limited not by their place of birth or the colour of their skin, but by the size of their hope".

"Having no parents or brothers, nor sisters of her own, she had no memories of childhood to treasure. Now at the point of her ultimate glory, her old age has been stolen from her as well. We have all lost a shining star".

Rupert was also devastated but he held it well. Vivian and Napoleon sandwiched him between them, trying their best to console him through their own deep grief.

At last, it was allover and they all departed from the cemetery to nurse their loss separately.

As the small crowd dispersed, no one noticed the lone figure of Dr Kalu, disappearing into his Nissan Caprice saloon car and slowly driving away.

He still could not make sense of it all. Since hearing of Angelou's death three days back, he had been stricken with a guilty conscience the size of a mountain.

He believed he brought it on her. If only he had known this was how it would end.

A week after the wedding, Vivian received a call in her office.

The friend at Telkom had traced the number she gave him. It was indeed a fax line and it belonged to an office inside the University of Johannesburg.

The office was in the department of History and it was occupied by one Kalu Nnanna.

Vivian thanked him and wondered aloud.

Wasn't that the new lecturer from Nigeria? Did he know Angelou? Was he connected with her death in anyway?

She picked up the phone and called the history department, asking the receptionist that spoke to her, to connect her to Dr Kalu.

The lady offered her apologies, explaining that the said Dr Kalu was no more with the department. That he had suddenly withdrawn from his sabbatical and resigned from all commitments with the department. He had cited a pressing, personal emergency back home and had vacated his apartment in town.

"So how can I get him now?", Vivian enquired hopefully.

"Well, he talked about returning to Nigeria immediately, so I believe he should have left".

"Oh that's unfortunate", she couldn't hide her disappointment. "Anyway thank you very much for your help".

Vivian sat there thinking hard and extensively that the departed Dr Kalu had been connected somehow with the events that surrounded their late friend's sudden suicide. But how on earth could that connection ever be established?

Her reverie was broken by an incoming call. She snatched the receiver off the hook.

"Yes?", her voice betraying her anxiety.

"Oh it's me Vivian", Rupert responded at the other end.

"Oh, how are you doing? Nice I believe?", she was surprised.

"I'm okay, thank you. I just wanted to let you know that I received a call from a solicitor's chambers here in town. They asked if I was Rupert Mabizela and when I confirmed it, they said I had to come to their offices in respect of a will left with them by Angelou. When I got there, they confirmed my identity once more and gave me a copy of the will to read. In it, I realized Angelou had left all her savings to me and the total of it was R16,788,009 million, not including a parcel of land she just bought at Empangeni. I'm confused Vivian. So much money!".

Vivian also didn't know what to say. Her huge hands wrapped around the receiver in a fierce grip. Neither her nor Maria in their wildest thoughts knew Angelou was so well-heeled.

"Are you still there?", Rupert asked.

"Yes I am. Whao! What a treasure you now have! That was really kind of Angel!", she managed to say.

"No Vivian, it isn't all for me. There was a proviso at the end in which she instructed that I would only have it as long as I agreed to split the amount in three ways with you and Maria. She wrote that two of you were all the family she had. Please don't argue with me. That is what she wanted and that is exactly what I intend to do".

Vivian was now even more shocked than the first time.

Before she could say anything, the line suddenly got cut off and only a dull beep sailed through to her ears.

What a woman Angelou was! What a friend! Oh what a companion they had all lost!

Of their own accord, her eyes filled over gradually and a steady stream of tears poured out slowly.

Tears of admiration and respect for a woman who had walked into all their lives without fanfare, but left it much better than she had met it.

Still weeping silently, she picked up the phone and dialed Maria's number to break the news to her.

As she waited for her friend to pick up the phone, her eyes couldn't help straying outside the window; across the wide courtyard and far ahead into the distance where she could see the freshly-inscribed legend: **Angelou Fanteni Department of Dramatic Arts**, boldly painted on the wall of the huge block of the department of Dramatic Arts.

It was part of the school's tribute to a woman who had won hearts and minds everywhere she had been. It was the first-ever mark of respect of its kind given to a non-native of South Africa by the institution.

It was the least they could do to honour the fallen head of the bereaved department.

A true woman of substance.

THE END.

ABOUT THE AUTHOR

Emma Nwaneri was born in 1970 in southeastern Nigeria four months after the end of the bitterly fought Nigerian Civil War. The second of ten children, he lost his mother when he was just eight, forcing his father to remarry.

Though an average student, he progressed through school speedily and completed his high school at just fifteen years of age. Even at that early age, his passion for reading and writing was becoming obvious. Of note was his award of best student in English literature of which he was given Thomas Hardy's Mayor of Casterbridge as prize.

He proceeded to further his education by studying mass communication at the University of Maiduguri, graduating in 1992.

Since then, he has worked full-time as a print journalist with special interest in sports reporting. He rose to become the sports editor of Nigerian Tribune, the oldest privately owned newspaper in sub-Saharan Africa by 1999.

The following year, he covered the 2000 Sydney Olympics games in Australia and later lived and worked in that country for three years.

He returned to Nigeria in 2003 and has since worked for various media outlets in Nigeria, Ghana, and the United

States of America. He currently lives in Johannesburg, South Africa, with his family.

He developed inspiration for writing from reading the works of Dennis Wheatley, Chinua Achebe, Zulu Sofola, James Hadley Chase, and Robert Ludlum.

He speaks three languages, and his dream remains to own a twenty-four-hour all-sports television network.

"Once Upon a Woman" is his second book.

Printed in the United States
By Bookmasters